BILLIONAIRE BOYS CLUB IN LOVE

CARA MILLER

Want my unreleased 5000-word story
Introducing the Billionaire Boys Club
and other free gifts from time to time?

Then join my mailing list at

http://www.caramillerbooks.com/inner-circle/

Subscribe now and read it now!

You can also follow me on Twitter and Facebook

Books in the Billionaire Romance Series:

The Billionaire Boys Club
Surrender to the Billionaire Boys Club
Billionaire Boys Club in New York
Summer with the Billionaire Boys Club
Secrets of the Billionaire Boys Club
A Date with the Billionaire Boys Club
Billionaire Boys Club in Love
Fireworks with the Billionaire Boys Club
An Evening with the Billionaire Boys Club
A Very Billionaire Boys Club Christmas
An Invitation from the Billionaire Boys Club
Midnight with the Billionaire Boys Club
Dreaming with the Billionaire Boys Club
A Promise from the Billionaire Boys Club
Engaged to the Billionaire Boys Club
A Surprise from the Billionaire Boys Club
Romance with the Billionaire Boys Club
A Billionaire Boys Club Wedding

Jessica was about to leave Darrow, Ryan, and Kelsey. Life would not be the same without her.

Jessica opened the door to their apartment, and she and Kelsey walked in. They had walked right past the boys' apartment, but they had heard no noise. Kelsey didn't know if that meant that Ryan was too devastated to talk right now, or if he hadn't returned to the apartment yet.

Jessica sat on the sofa, and Kelsey sat next to her.

"Do you want to talk?" Kelsey asked. Jessica shook her head, and her ponytail swung.

"There's nothing to talk about. Ryan wanted to know, and I told him. Now he knows," Jessica said without emotion.

"Jess...." Kelsey began. But she didn't know what to say. She put her arms around Jessica's shoulders, and willed herself not to cry.

Jessica said she was going to bed early, but the light stayed on in her room hours after she had closed the door. Kelsey finally went to bed herself at midnight, but —as she suspected was true for Jessica and Ryan as well — she was unable to sleep.

Tyler didn't come to the gym the next morning. After Jessica's bombshell announcement to Ryan that she was leaving, Kelsey knew that Ryan would have kept Tyler up all night to talk.

Kelsey walked back into her apartment after her workout, and was surprised to see that Jessica was up. Jessica looked radiant, as if she had had a good night's sleep and was at peace, a stark contrast to the previous week.

"Good morning, Kels," Jessica said brightly. She was already showered and dressed, her auburn curls in her usual ponytail.

"Hey," Kelsey said.

"Come with me. I want to go over to talk to the boys," Jessica replied.

"Okay," Kelsey said. She took her shower and got dressed. With her damp hair pinned up on top of her head, she and Jessica left their apartment and walked down the hall. Jessica opened the boys' apartment door with her key.

A very sleepy looking Tyler met them at the door.

"Morning," he said, giving Kelsey a kiss as Jessica walked into the apartment. Ryan, who never seemed to need much sleep, sat with his legs up on the sofa, while Zachary slept on a pillow on the living room floor.

Jessica walked over and sat next to Ryan, who put his arm around her. Tyler and Kelsey sat on the surrounding chairs. Zach continued to sleep.

"I'm staying here," Jessica said simply. "I'm not going back to New York."

Kelsey looked at Jessica in surprise.

"You said that your parents said you had to," Ryan said.

"They did. But I thought all night about what you said yesterday. That I needed to do what was right for me. Staying at Darrow is the right thing to do. I don't want to transfer now. I want to finish."

"What will your parents say?" Tyler asked Jessica.

"I don't know. All I know is that I'm going to stay in Seattle."

"Are you sure?" Ryan asked. Jessica nodded and Ryan hugged her. Jessica looked at Kelsey, who was beaming.

"We're going to have to find a cheap apartment this summer. I'm going to have to save my money for tuition next year," Jessica said.

"You can live with us," Ryan said, hugging her tighter.

"I don't think so."

"Oh, come on. We're great roommates. Tell her, Kelsey," Ryan said.

Kelsey laughed. "Tyler and Ryan are excellent roommates. I had a wonderful time last summer."

"See. You can live rent-free," Ryan said.

Jessica stroked his face with his hand. "I'll think about it," she said. She rested her head against Ryan's shoulder and closed her eyes peacefully.

The next afternoon, Kelsey joined Tyler on a trip to Professor Bell's office hours.

"I've been putting it off for a while," Tyler said. Kelsey knew why. Professor Bell was absolutely tedious. But if they were going to try to figure out how to prepare for Professor Bell's exam, they needed to talk to the expert.

"Here goes," Tyler said, doubtfully, knocking on the door.

"Come in," Professor Bell said happily. Kelsey guessed that not too many people visited Professor Bell, afraid that they'd be trapped for hours listening to him expound on the wonders of trademark law. Professor Bell was rather long-winded.

Tyler and Kelsey entered Professor Bell's office. There were books and stacks of paper everywhere. On the bookshelves, stacked on the floor, lining the window. Even covering the desk. Kelsey wondered how he got anything done.

"Mr. Olsen, Miss North. Sit, sit," Professor Bell said with glee. Kelsey had to remind herself that she had willingly walked into office hours, because she felt like she had walked into a trap.

"Hello, Professor," Tyler said charmingly.

"It's wonderful to see you! Are you here to discuss the upcoming article in the Darrow Law Review analyzing the Supreme Court decision about *B&B Hardware, Inc. v. Hargis Industries, Inc.* ? It's quite an interesting case…"

A half hour later, Professor Bell finally stopped talking. He looked at Tyler and Kelsey as if he had just realized that they were sitting there.

"So," he said, "why did you come to visit?" he asked brightly.

"To find out what was on the exam," Tyler said pointedly.

"Oh!" Professor Bell said cheerfully. "I'll be testing you on *Hormel Foods Corp. v. Spam Arrest, LLC*. It's a trademark cancellation case from 2007. You'll be asked to analyze the Trademark Trial and Appeal Board's decision."

Kelsey looked at him in complete surprise.

"Although we know exactly what our exam is on, I'm wondering whether it was worth it," Tyler said a half hour later, as they sat in the library cafe.

"Did he actually just tell us what to study?" Kelsey said. She couldn't believe that Professor Bell had been so forthcoming about the exam. He had practically given them the questions.

"I guess so," Tyler said.

"Why?" Kelsey asked.

"Probably because we asked him. My guess is not too many people go to Professor Bell's office hours."

"Now we know why," Kelsey said.

"Another professor for the 'must avoid' list?" Tyler teased.

"Yes, but Professor Eliot remains in the top spot," Kelsey replied.

"Now we know what to work on," Tyler said. "This is going to save us a lot of time. That should make up for the hour we wasted listening to him talk about a Darrow Law Review article. At least it wasn't one I worked on."

"That's a plus."

"So if we know what to study for Bell, and we're ready for Negotiation, then we just need to work on Securities 2, and Zach can help with that," Tyler said.

"What do you mean, 'we're ready for Negotiation?'" Kelsey said. She didn't feel ready at all.

"You'll be fine," Tyler said.

On Saturday afternoon, Kelsey walked into the apartment. She had spent the morning in the library with Tyler, studying the Hormel Foods case for the Trademarks exam.

Jessica was sitting at the kitchen table, her computer in front of her, talking on Skype. Kelsey noticed that video was off and a box of tissues sat next to the computer.

"Jessica Leigh," a male voice that Kelsey recognized as Jessica's father — Dr. Hunter — said, "I've told you that we're not paying for another year at Darrow."

"I know," Jessica said. She gestured for Kelsey to sit in the seat next to her. Kelsey joined her.

"You know. Then why haven't you begun applying to transfer?"

"Daddy, I'm not transferring," Jessica said.

"I don't understand," her father replied.

"I've always done everything you've wanted me to do. But I earned my spot here, and I don't want to leave."

"Is this because of that boy?" her father asked.

"No. It's because I want to graduate from Darrow."

"You can graduate from Columbia or NYU just as easily."

"No, Daddy," Jessica said.

"Did you just say no to me?" Mr. Hunter said gruffly.

Jessica swallowed meekly, but found her voice. "I did, Daddy," she said.

"Do you understand what you're doing, Jessica?"

"Yes. I'm disobeying you," Jessica replied.

There was silence. Jessica picked up one of the tissues and dabbed at her eyes.

"Fine," Dr. Hunter said sharply. And the line went dead.

At Sunday brunch in the dining hall the next day, Jessica's phone rang. Thinking it was her own, Kelsey glanced at the readout, which read 'Daddy'. Jessica reached over and silenced the phone.

Over the next two days as they were studying for exams, Kelsey noticed that Jessica got several calls where she would glance at the readout, then silence the phone. But on the third day, the phone calls stopped.

Kelsey sat across a table from Tyler, who was smiling at her. This was the scenario that she was dreading, but she needed to face it.

"Ready, Miss North?" Tyler asked her.

"No," she replied.

"Let's start then. Negotiations are always better if the other party is unprepared."

"I'm not unprepared. I'm just not ready," Kelsey countered.

"Do I intimidate you?" Tyler asked.

"A little," Kelsey admitted.

Tyler smiled. "Even better for me then," he said brightly.

"If I get you to negotiate against in the exam, I'm just standing up and leaving," Kelsey said.

"Then I win," Tyler said. "Do you really want that?"

"No," Kelsey admitted.

"Then let's begin again," Tyler said. "Are you ready?" he repeated.

"Yes," Kelsey said, looking into his brown eyes with determination.

The Thursday before exams and a few days after Jessica's call with her father, Jessica got a call on Skype. Kelsey looked up from her book. She could see that the call was from Andrea Hunter.

Jessica sighed, then answered the call. Andrea, Jessica's sister-in-law, appeared on screen.

"Jessie. Are you okay?"

"I'm fine," Jessica responded.

"Nana and I have been so worried about you."

"Sorry," Jessica said.

"It's okay. I know that you're busy."

"Yeah, I have exams next week. How are things there?"

Andrea sighed. She looked tired.

"You know that your father is furious."

"I know."

"Joey offered to go out to Seattle and drag you back to New York. I'm not sure he was kidding, but your father said that you needed to come back on your own. He's expecting you to come back for spring break."

"I'm not coming."

"He doesn't believe that you're going to continue to defy him," Andrea said bluntly. "Jess, I'm a Hunter by marriage, not by birth, so I don't agree with what's going on. I love and support you."

"Thanks," Jessica replied.

"Your mother does too, although she's not going to say anything against your father," Andrea said. Jessica nodded, but didn't speak.

"Do you need anything?" Andrea asked.

"I'm fine."

"Hang on," Andrea said. She walked away from the camera, and Jessica's nephew Nick came on screen.

"Hi, Aunt Jess!" he said brightly.

"Hi, Sunshine," Jessica answered back.

"I miss you, Aunt Jess. When are you coming back?"

"Not for a while," Jessica said. Kelsey could hear the catch in Jessica's voice.

"Aww," Nick said. "Really?"

"I need to finish school, Nick."

"Okay," Nick said. "Did you know I got a new set of Legos?" he asked her.

"No, I didn't know that," Jessica replied.

"Oh, okay. Bye, Aunt Jess!" Nick said.

"I love you," Jessica said, as Nick disappeared from the screen and Andrea returned.

"Jessie, I need to start dinner. Make sure you send me a message every so often so I know you're okay. Are you sure you don't need anything?"

"I'm fine, Andrea. Thanks."

"All right. You tell your cute troublemaker boyfriend hello. I know he's the reason that you're standing up to your father," Jessica laughed.

"He's not, but okay," she said.

"Bye, Jess," Andrea said, and she disconnected.

Tuesday was Kelsey's first exam, and it was Negotiation. To her relief, she was paired with Erica, who was a capable but not stellar negotiator. Jessica was paired with Alana Alexander, who despite her reputation for being ditzy, was actually an excellent negotiator. Kelsey thought Jess's work was cut out for her.

But no one was in as much trouble as Ryan. He had been paired with Tyler.

"Is this a joke?" Kelsey heard Ryan comment petulantly as she took her seat across the table from Erica.

"Yes. For me," Tyler replied, smiling.

On Wednesday morning, to Kelsey's surprise and utter delight, the Trademarks exam was almost exactly as Professor Bell had said during office hours. She felt almost guilty, until Tyler pointed out at lunch that everyone in class could have done what they did and asked Professor Bell directly. He suggested that she enjoy the A she was likely to get.

Thursday night, they all sat in the boys' apartment studying Securities. Tyler and Zach had written the outline together.

"Are you really going to do this for the rest of your life?" Ryan said to Zach, putting aside the outline and snuggling next to Jessica. They had been told that the exam would focus on examining annual reports and financial statements.

"That's what I've been told," Zach said.

"You don't care?" Ryan asked.

"Not really," Zach said.

"Why are you even in law school?" Jessica asked Zach curiously.

"So my parents can stop paying their law firm so much money to analyze contracts and legal statements of the companies they are considering investing in," Zach said.

"Makes sense," Jessica said.

"Of course it does. They won't be paying me five hundred dollars an hour," Zach replied.

"Why don't they just hire a staff lawyer?" Jessica asked.

"The work comes in waves, and my mother hates to see people sitting around with little to do," Zach said.

"Your mother is picky," Ryan said.

"She is," Zach said.

"About everything. And everyone," Ryan continued. Kelsey knew he was referring to Kim.

"We have an exam tomorrow, Ryan," Tyler warned.

Zach looked at Ryan with his dark eyes.

"I cannot control my parents, Ryan," Zach said. "No more than you can control Bob, or Tyler can control Lisa. All I can do is try to get around their rules."

Ryan sighed, but said nothing more.

On Friday night, exams were over. Zach had already left campus, off to two weeks in Cabo San Lucas with some friends from Princeton. Kim was off on a shoot in Morocco, so they wouldn't be spending this spring break together. Ryan was cooking dinner for Jessica in the boys' apartment. And Tyler and Kelsey were sitting in a booth at a restaurant in Ballard, kissing.

"We should order," Kelsey said, pulling away from Tyler and picking up her menu.

"I know what I want," Tyler said.

"I bet," Kelsey said.

Tyler grinned. He got up and sat across from Kelsey. "Pad Thai," Tyler commented. "With chicken. How about you?"

"Basil fried rice. And a thai iced tea."

"Make it two," Tyler said. He gently took the menu from her hands.

"I'm looking forward to getting you out into the wilderness," Kelsey said.

"You make it sound like a threat," Tyler said.

"I'll be interested to see your reaction," Kelsey said.

"I liked Port Townsend," Tyler said.

"Port Townsend is a town. We'll be in the woods."

"Sounds romantic," Tyler said looking at her.

"Does it?" Kelsey asked.

Tyler shrugged. "It does to me," he replied.

"Studying for exams sounds romantic to you," Kelsey commented wryly.

"I get to be with you. What could be more romantic than that?" Tyler asked her, taking her hand and kissing it.

"The preppy goes camping," Ryan commented the next day as Tyler placed his bag into the trunk of Tyler's Audi.

Tyler glanced at him. "Camping is a prep sport," he replied.

"Perhaps, but it's like you stepped out of the L.L. Bean catalog. You're the perfect WASP."

Tyler laughed. "Jeffrey packed for me. I doubt he's been camping, so he probably had to use the Bean catalog to figure out what I needed."

"I think Tyler looks great," Jessica said. "It's exactly what I expected. Rugged and lots of flannel."

Kelsey smiled. She was wearing her ripped jeans and a dark fleece jacket. "I didn't realize there was a camping look."

Jessica raised an eyebrow. "That's because you wear it 24-7."

Kelsey giggled. "I look like everyone else in Seattle."

"And everyone in Seattle dresses like they're going camping," Jessica commented.

"Everyone can't be as fabulous as New Yorkers," Kelsey teased.

"True," Jessica said, tossing her hair.

"Then again, you're going to freeze to death if you don't bring another jacket," Kelsey said, looking at Jessica.

"It's cold?" Ryan asked in concern.

"We don't camp in a building," Tyler replied.

"We'll have a tent," Ryan retorted.

"Tents aren't heated," Kelsey said.

"We'll have a fire, right?" Ryan asked.

"Not at night," Kelsey said.

Ryan looked at her. "I'm going to get another jacket," he said.

"Me, too," Jessica agreed. Ryan and Jessica walked back into the apartment building together.

Tyler smiled at Kelsey.

"So do I have everything I need, Miss North?" he asked her.

Kelsey looked in the trunk of the car. Jeffrey certainly seemed to have outfitted Tyler with everything he could possibly use in the wild. She saw that there were three clear plastic tubs in the trunk, in addition to Tyler's new duffel bag.

The tubs held sturdy hiking boots, an extra fleece jacket, warm socks, and a blanket, in addition to lots of camping-friendly snacks. The blanket caught Kelsey's eye, and she opened the tub and pulled it out.

"Pendleton?" she said, turning the brand new, thick wool blanket around in her hands. It was beautiful, navy with Hudson Bay stripes.

"Tyler, do you know how much this blanket costs?" Kelsey asked.

Tyler shrugged.

"Of course not," Kelsey said, refolding the three-hundred-dollar blanket and placing it neatly back into the plastic tub. "Well, at least you'll be warm," she commented as Ryan and Jessica returned, both holding fleece jackets.

"We will be, too," Ryan said brightly. "Are we ready?"

"I think so," Kelsey said with sarcasm. "In fact, I think we could plan on moving out into the wilderness permanently with all of this stuff."

"Jeffrey likes us to be prepared," Tyler said to her.

"Obviously. But there's a store approximately thirty yards from the campsite. I think we'll survive," Kelsey replied.

"We don't want to just survive. We want to be comfortable," Ryan said.

"That's not why you go camping," Kelsey commented.

"And that's why we're going to the city of Portland next," Jessica said. "Are you sure this is going to be fun?" she asked.

Ryan hugged her. "Of course it will. We'll be together. And if it gets too cold we'll sleep in the RV."

Kelsey sighed. Tyler looked at her and laughed.

"Are we already upsetting you? We haven't even left Seattle," he asked her.

"I guess I forgot that I was surrounded by city people," she responded.

"I bet you'll remember after one night in the wilderness," Tyler replied.

"Are there bears?" Ryan wondered. "I forgot to ask."

"Bears?" Jessica asked in terror.

"Doubtful," Kelsey said. "Not at Fort Flagler. The most deadly animals are probably the deer."

"Deer? Deer are harmless. Aren't they?" Jessica asked nervously.

"Not if you run into them with your speeding car," Kelsey said.

"Oh, that will be a problem," Tyler said, looking at Ryan.

"I'll slow up," Ryan replied.

"Hardly," Tyler said.

"Are we ready?" Jessica said. "I want to get this over with."

"Jess, we're going to be there for five nights," Kelsey said.

"Worst case, we'll move into a hotel in Port Townsend," Ryan said comfortingly to Jessica.

"There are hotels in Port Townsend?" Jessica asked.

"Yes, Jess. And it's only a half hour away," Kelsey said. "Maybe we should just camp in my parents' backyard."

"Don't give up on us yet, Miss North," Tyler said. "We're teachable."

"I hope so," Kelsey said doubtfully.

Despite giving Tyler a fifteen-minute head start, Ryan and Jessica reached the Edmonds ferry first. Kelsey saw the silver Porsche fly by on I-5 as they passed by Northgate Mall. They got in the ferry line, and both cars somehow managed to get on the same ferry to Kingston.

They met up in the seating area upstairs and chatted while the ferry crossed the sound. Per Kelsey's request, once they drove off the ferry, they parked and walked around downtown Kingston, Washington.

Kelsey's mother had asked Kelsey to buy a new pair of scissors from the fabric store, and after purchasing them, and buying chocolate-and-whipped-cream-filled crepes, the group walked over to the waterfront park next to the ferry landing.

"This is gorgeous," Jessica enthused as they walked around the park, eating their crepes. The sun was shining brightly as they walked on the green grass.

"It's cold," Ryan complained.

"You have no idea how cold it's going to get," Tyler commented. Ryan frowned at him.

"Maybe you should consider moving to California," Kelsey said to Ryan.

"Would you go, Jess?" Ryan asked her.

Jessica shook her head. "No seasons," she replied.

"Then no," Ryan said to Kelsey. Kelsey took a bite of her crepe.

"Then I guess you'll freeze with us here in Washington State," Tyler said to Ryan.

Ryan sighed.

"It needs to be summer again," Ryan said.

They arrived in Port Hadlock after a short drive from Kingston, and stopped by the large QFC grocery store.

Ryan got a large grocery cart and Kelsey looked at him.

"What are you doing?" she asked.

"Buying groceries for dinner," Ryan replied.

"You need a cart?" Kelsey asked.

"I'm cooking Brazilian," Ryan said.

"What? We're camping," Kelsey said.

"I know, but I wanted something normal for dinner," Ryan replied.

"Brazilian food is normal?" Kelsey asked.

"Sure," Ryan said nonchalantly.

"Okay," Kelsey said doubtfully. She bit her lip. "Where are you going to cook all of this? Over the campfire?"

"Don't be silly. In the kitchen," Ryan said.

"Kitchen?"

"The RV. Dad is meeting us," Ryan answered.

"Right, of course," Kelsey said. She looked at him puzzled. "The RV has a kitchen big enough to cook a gourmet meal?"

"You'll see," Ryan said, wheeling the cart off, with Jessica walking next to him. "Jess, do you have my list?" Kelsey heard him say. Jessica pulled a large sheet of paper out of her bag, and although Ryan and Jessica were almost out of sight, Kelsey could have sworn the list covered the page.

"Do you want to go buy dessert, Kels?" Tyler asked her. Kelsey looked at him, almost startled that he was there. "Ryan put us in charge of desserts and snacks."

Kelsey looked at Tyler in interest.

"You guys do realize that we're camping? Living the way our ancestors did? Roughing it?" Kelsey said.

"I don't think any of us got that memo," Tyler said.

"That seems pretty clear," Kelsey said.

"So what do you want for dessert?"

"S'mores. It's the only dessert for camping," Kelsey replied.

"Are you a purist, Miss North? Because I think Jessica wanted tiramisu," Tyler said.

Kelsey sighed.

"Get whatever you want," she said in defeat.

A half hour later, Ryan was done with his shopping, and he and Tyler were loading seven grocery bags into the car. Kelsey looked at the foot-long receipt in Jessica's hand.

"Well, we certainly won't starve," Kelsey commented.

"How far is the campground from here?" Ryan asked, as Tyler placed the last of the bags into the Audi.

"Fifteen minutes," Kelsey shrugged. "Why?"

"I'll need to come back tomorrow," Ryan said. Tyler closed the door of the trunk.

"Why?"

"Groceries," Ryan said, as if it were obvious.

"We have seven bags of groceries," Kelsey pointed out.

"Dinner, breakfast and lunch at most," Ryan said.

"Right. Okay," Kelsey said in disbelief.

"There's almost a full bag of herbs and spices," Jessica said to Kelsey.

"When we go camping, we have hot dogs," Kelsey said.

"Gross," Ryan said. "Come on, let's go." Ryan and Jessica got into Ryan's car and Kelsey and Tyler got into the Audi.

Tyler drove behind Ryan, who was driving slower than usual. Kelsey assumed he had seen the police car parked outside of QFC. They drove along the curvy road through Port Hadlock, through Indian Island and onto Marrowstone Island, at the tip of which lay their destination.

Tyler drove slowly as they reached the tiny village of Nordland. They passed a general store with an American flag outside, a small cafe and a harbor with about twenty boats.

"Beautiful," Tyler said, as they passed a group of sailboats anchored on the water. "It's like small town Americana."

They continued their drive up to the state park, eventually turning left onto the campground road. After a check-in at the booth, they drove into the park.

"What's that?" Tyler asked as they drove past a set of concrete structures.

"Old bunkers," Kelsey said. "This used to be a fort."

"Can we go in them?" Tyler asked.

"Of course. We can walk around later. They hold concerts over there in the summer," Kelsey said as Tyler drove on. They reached the lower campground and followed Ryan to their camping space. As they parked, Kelsey saw her dad sitting with Ryan's dad outside an enormous vehicle, which Kelsey assumed was Bob's RV.

Her dad stood up from his camp chair as Kelsey got out of Tyler's car.

"Kels!" he said happily. She ran into his arms as Tyler greeted Bob. Mr. North hugged Kelsey, then shook Tyler's hand.

"Nice to see you, Tyler," Mr. North said.

"You too, Dan," Tyler replied with a grin.

"Hi, Bob," Kelsey said.

"Thank you for inviting me, Kelsey," Bob said. "I was telling your father I haven't been camping in years."

"We'll have fun," Kelsey said, glancing over at Ryan, who was directing the unloading of grocery bags from Tyler's car. Tyler had gone over to help.

"I brought your tents as requested, Kels," her father said to her. "I brought the six-person tent as well as a four-person one. I also brought the screen house, so you can cover the picnic table." Mr. North glanced at the RV. "But I'm not sure you'll have room."

"I'll make it work," Kelsey said. "Thanks, Dad."

"Are you staying for dinner?" Tyler asked, walking over. He had helped Ryan carry the groceries into the RV.

"I need to get back to the store," Mr. North said. Jessica and Ryan walked over.

"Hi, Mr. North," Jessica said.

"Jessica, it's great to see you," Mr. North said.

"This is my son, Ryan," Bob said. Mr. North stuck out his hand, and

Ryan shook it.

"Nice to meet you. I've heard a lot about you," Mr. North said. Ryan glanced uneasily at Kelsey.

"Wasn't me," Kelsey giggled.

"Dan and I have had a nice talk while we were waiting for you," Bob said, smiling at his son.

"We stopped in Port Hadlock," Kelsey said, by way of explanation. She had sent her father a text earlier from the ferry. "I hope you weren't here too long."

"It's fine, Kels. Your mother's in the store."

"Oh, right," Kelsey said, dashing back to the car, and retrieving the bag from the fabric store. "This is for Mom."

"Great, she said you had something for her," Mr. North said. "I'll let you guys get settled. Jasmine and Morgan are coming over later?"

"Yep," Kelsey said excitedly.

"Need any help putting up the tent?" Mr. North asked.

"You know I don't," Kelsey replied.

Mr. North grinned.

"Better tell Tyler," he said.

Kelsey glanced around at Tyler, who was picking up one of the tent holders.

"Hey, touch nothing," Kelsey warned.

"Why?" Tyler asked her curiously, as she walked over and removed the tent poles from his hand.

"Kelsey is in charge of putting up the tent," Mr. North said in amusement.

"I'd like to know who else is going to," Kelsey commented.

"I can help," Tyler said.

"No," Kelsey replied sharply.

"Kelsey's been doing it by herself since she was fifteen," Mr. North commented.

"It's too confusing with everyone moving pieces around," Kelsey said. "I'll do it."

"I can't help?" Tyler asked her.

"You can watch if you're quiet," Kelsey said. Tyler looked at Mr. North, who shrugged.

"Just let her do it. It's not worth fighting about," Mr. North said. Tyler smiled at Kelsey.

"Okay, Miss North. I'll let you do what you do best," he said.

"Thank you," Kelsey said.

"All right, kids. I'll head on. Have fun. Bob, it was great meeting you."

"Same here." Bob and Mr. North shook hands. Kelsey gave her father another hug, tent poles still in her hand.

"Bye, Dad," she said. Dan shook Tyler's hand again, waved at the rest and walked over to his truck. He got in, started it and drove off, as Kelsey began looking through the equipment that her father had left on the ground in their camping space. As he had said, there were two tents and a cover, and he had also left a large box filled with sleeping bags, blankets, and pillows.

Ryan and Jessica returned to the RV, while Bob sat in one of the camping chairs and Tyler took the other.

"So what dirt do you have on Ryan?" Bob asked Kelsey. Kelsey glanced at Bob.

"She dated Ryan first," Tyler said to him, frowning at Kelsey, who grinned and went back to sorting out the tent.

"I see," Bob said, amused.

"It's fine," Kelsey said, pulling the first set of tent poles out of the bag, and glancing at the instructions.

"No, it's not," Tyler said to her.

"Of course it is. It was two dates," Kelsey replied. Bob took a drink from a cup that had been sitting on the ground next to his chair.

"Who dumped who?" Bob asked Tyler.

"It was a tie," Tyler replied.

Kelsey scowled at him. "I dumped Ryan," she said to Bob.

"You shouldn't have gone out with him," Tyler said, matter-of-factly.

"No one else had asked me out," Kelsey retorted.

"You should have waited," Tyler replied.

"Do you want a tent? Or would you rather sleep on the ground?" Kelsey threatened.

"A tent, please," Tyler replied, grinning.

"Then shut up about me and Ryan," Kelsey said with a smile.

Bob took another drink.

"How's school?" Bob asked.

"Stressful," Tyler replied as Kelsey began to assemble the poles.

"It's good," Kelsey said.

"A difference of opinion?" Bob asked.

"I'm not on Law Review," Kelsey said.

"Yeah, that would make a difference," Bob said. "How do you think Ryan did this term?" he asked Tyler.

"Good," Tyler said confidently. "He's been studying a lot."

"Jessica's influence?" Bob asked.

"Probably," Tyler agreed.

"He's serious about her?"

"Very," Tyler replied as Kelsey began carefully threading the poles through the tent.

"Why?" Bob asked.

Tyler didn't answer for a moment.

"I think because she wants what Ryan wants," he finally said.

"Which is?" Bob asked.

"A family. Stability," Tyler replied.

"I see," Bob said. "What happened to his wrist in New York?"

Kelsey saw Tyler shake his head.

"I can't tell you," Tyler said.

"You'd rather I guess?" Bob said.

"I'm afraid so," Tyler replied.

"Ryan wouldn't tell me either. But I saw the charges from the Mercer, so I'm going to guess it wasn't a good visit with the Hunters," Bob said. Tyler was silent.

"Fine. Be loyal," Bob said. "I'm glad Ryan has you. You keep him out of trouble."

Tyler laughed. "No, I don't."

"Ryan is capable of much more damage than he's caused over the years. I give you credit."

"I don't think it's deserved," Tyler replied.

"He looks up to you," Bob said nonchalantly.

"No, he doesn't," Tyler replied as Kelsey began lifting the tent. He stood up.

"Can I help?" Tyler asked her.

"No. Shush," Kelsey said.

Bob looked at her in amusement. "It's very zen, putting up a tent," he commented. Tyler sat back down.

"You have a good head on your shoulders. I appreciate that," Bob said to Tyler.

"Hmm," Tyler said.

"How's Chris?" Bob asked.

"I was wondering when you'd get to that," Tyler said wryly.

"Lisa wasn't amused by my Super Bowl stunt," Bob said.

"I didn't think she would be," Tyler commented. "How did she find out?"

"Chris's lawyers, I think," Bob said. "He wasn't amused either."

"My parents are a lot alike," Tyler said.

"That's why they hate each other," Bob replied. "You should make up with Chris."

"I know," Tyler said. "Later."

"Still angry?"

"Yes."

"Chris shouldn't have used you like that, but he's never gotten over Lisa outsmarting him," Bob said.

"She's smarter than him," Tyler said, watching as Kelsey drove the tent picks into the ground. She was almost done assembling the first tent.

"Don't tell him that," Bob commented.

"I know. I won't," Tyler replied. Ryan came out of the RV, holding two glasses filled with a green goo.

"What's this?" Bob asked him.

"Vitamina de abacate," Ryan said, handing one of the glasses to Bob and one to Tyler. "Avocado smoothie."

"No, thanks," Bob said handing the glass back to Ryan.

"Try it," Ryan pouted.

"Forget it," Bob replied.

"You won't try anything," Ryan said.

Bob smiled at the look on Ryan's face. "I grew up on meat and potatoes, Ryan. I'm not drinking that," Bob said.

"Just because it's green doesn't mean it isn't good," Ryan retorted.

"The only green things I'm eating are peas," Bob replied.

"You're missing out," Ryan said.

"Make it for Lisa. She loves that kind of crap," Bob said.

"Kels, do you want to try it?" Ryan asked her, taking the glass over. Kelsey was standing, admiring her handiwork. The first tent was up perfectly.

"Sure," Kelsey said. She took the glass and had a sip. "Nice," she said in surprise. It was a sweet avocado milkshake.

"It is good," Tyler said.

"It's a traditional Brazilian drink," Ryan said proudly.

"Is that what you're cooking tonight?" Bob asked him. "Brazilian?"

"Yes," Ryan said. "Lots of meat," he added petulantly. He walked back into the RV.

"How long has he been cooking?" Bob asked Tyler.

"Since last summer."

"The things he thinks up," Bob said, shaking his head.

Kelsey proceeded to put up the second, smaller tent as Tyler and Bob continued to chat.

"Lisa wants you to work for her this summer. She doesn't like you working for Simon," Bob said to him.

"Because she hates Simon?" Tyler guessed.

"Because she loves you. She really wants you to work for her."

"I know," Tyler said. "But once I start working for Tactec, I won't be able to leave."

"That's probably true."

"She'll wait. It's only one more summer," Tyler said. "Anyway, I'll be at all of the dozens of board meetings."

"There won't be as many this year, now that we have Chen Industries," Bob said.

"No?" Tyler asked. Bob shook his head.

"I don't think so," Bob said.

"Good. Simon was upset that I had to take so much time off," Tyler commented.

"Don't relax yet. I think your mother has something up her sleeve for you."

"What?" Tyler asked.

"If I knew, I'd tell you. I just know she's spent quite a bit of time plotting something with your man Jeffrey lately."

"Great," Tyler said with sarcasm.

"Done," Kelsey said happily. The second tent was up.

"Nice work, Miss North."

"Thank you, Mr. Olsen," Kelsey said.

"Can I go in?"

"Sure, but take off your shoes first," Kelsey said. Tyler stood up and walked over to the larger of the two tents. He left his shoes outside and stepped in. Kelsey took his seat next to Bob.

"So why did you break up with Ryan?" Bob asked, sipping his drink.

"Long story. It was over a year ago," Kelsey hedged.

"Where are you working this summer?"

"Collins Nicol," Kelsey said.

"Really? Which department?"

"IP."

"With Mary White?"

Kelsey nodded. "You know her?"

"I've met her," Bob replied.

"The tent's really awesome, Kels," Tyler said to her as he stepped out of the tent and back into his shoes.

"We just need to throw in the sleeping bags and we're all set," Kelsey replied.

"I can't wait. I've always wanted to sleep in a tent," Tyler said.

"Really? Why?" Bob asked.

"You don't think it would be fun?" Tyler said.

"Not really," Bob replied.

"You like the outdoors," Kelsey commented.

"I like my bed," Bob replied.

Ryan stepped out of the RV, holding a bowl of little rolls.

"And what are these?" Bob asked doubtfully.

"*Pao de queijo*. Cheese bread," Ryan said, handing him the bowl.

"I'll try that," Bob said, taking one of the rolls.

"I thought you might," Ryan replied. Bob passed the bowl to Kelsey, who took one of the rolls.

"This is great," Bob said, chewing. "What did you call it?"

"*Pao de queijo*," Ryan repeated. Kelsey bit into the soft cheese puff. It was amazing.

"Is it hard to make?" Bob asked, as Tyler reached into the bowl and took one.

"Easy," Ryan replied.

"How many can I eat?" Bob asked.

"As many as you want. I can make more," Ryan said.

"Thanks," Bob said, reaching back into the bowl and removing another puff. "So why did you and Kelsey break up?" he asked Ryan.

"Kelsey wouldn't sleep with me," Ryan replied nonchalantly. Kelsey looked at him in shock. She couldn't imagine saying that to one of her parents. But Bob didn't react. He took another bite of cheese bread.

"Good for you," Bob said to her, once he finished chewing. Kelsey wasn't sure what to say to that, so she ate another cheese puff. "What's Jessica doing?" Bob asked Ryan.

"Cutting vegetables," Ryan replied.

"When are we going to eat?" Bob asked him.

"In about an hour. Didn't you eat before you left Bellevue?" Ryan asked.

"I was in a meeting. I didn't have time," Bob said, taking another cheese puff. Ryan handed him the bowl.

"I'll put some more on," Ryan said.

"Thank you," Bob said, and Ryan went back into the RV.

"Why didn't you have Margaret make something for you?" Tyler asked Bob.

"Margaret is cooking a special dinner for Tim Mayer tonight," Bob said looking at Tyler meaningfully.

"Are you kidding me? I was hoping he was gone," Tyler said.

"Nope," Bob commented.

Tyler sighed.

"Mayer really, really wants the Chen Industries work," Bob mused, biting into a cheese puff.

"She's not going to give it to him, is she?" Tyler asked.

Bob shook his head. "No. But Tim's pretty upset about your mother giving it to Lindsay and Lewis, so she's trying to make amends." Bob paused. "What do you think of him?"

"Did Lisa ask you to ask me?"

"No, it's between you and me," Bob replied.

"I don't like him."

"Why?" Bob asked, finishing the cheese puff.

"Ryan called him slick. I think I agree with that assessment," Tyler replied.

"Yeah, Ryan doesn't like him at all. He told Lisa to dump him."

Tyler laughed. "When?"

"Every time Ryan sees her, I think," Bob said.

"Why does she like him?" Tyler asked Bob.

"I think your mother is lonely," Bob said. "Tim's a distraction."

"I wish she'd find a different one," Tyler said.

"Do you want me to set her up with someone else?" Bob asked.

"No, she'll get bored with him soon enough," Tyler said.

"That's probably true," Bob replied.

Kelsey took another cheese puff, and ate it thoughtfully. It was interesting watching Bob interact with the boys. It was like he was their peer, and not Ryan's father. No wonder Tyler didn't see Bob as a father figure.

Jessica left the RV with another bowl of cheese puffs, which she handed to Tyler.

"Ryan said you guys wanted more."

"They're delicious," Kelsey said.

"Don't fill up. Ryan's making an awesome main course," Jessica replied, returning to the RV.

"Give me the warm ones," Bob said to Tyler. They traded bowls. Bob took another cheese puff.

"Can I put the sleeping bags into the tent?" Tyler asked Kelsey. She glanced at his excited eyes.

"Sure," Kelsey said. Tyler handed her the second bowl of cheese puffs, then dragged the large box of sleeping bags over to the tent entrance. "Four for the big tent, two for the little one."

"Okay," Tyler said.

"Kelsey, where in Port Townsend do your parents live?"

"Do you know Port Townsend well?"

"Well enough."

"Near Uptown. A few blocks from the market," Kelsey replied.

"And the store's on Water Street?"

"Right."

"Have you lived here all of your life?"

"Except for college," Kelsey said.

"Where'd you go to school? Somewhere in Oregon, right?"

"Portland State," Kelsey replied.

"What's your major?"

"Biology," Kelsey replied.

Bob raised an eyebrow. "I wouldn't have pegged you as a scientist," he commented.

"She's quite smart," Tyler said, as he moved the bin from one tent to the other.

"I'm sure she is, if she's friends with you," Bob said.

"And what do you mean by that?" Tyler asked.

"It means you don't suffer fools gladly," Bob said.

"No, I guess I don't," Tyler replied, taking off his shoes and dragging a sleeping bag into the tent.

"Why did you go to law school if you majored in biology?" Bob asked Kelsey, eating another cheese puff.

"I always wanted to be a lawyer," Kelsey replied.

"Then why did you major in Biology? It isn't a natural fit for becoming a lawyer."

"I was good at it," Kelsey shrugged.

"Fair enough," Bob said.

Jessica left the RV.

"Is dinner ready?" Bob asked Jessica.

"Not yet," Jessica said, smiling at him.

"Tell Ryan to hurry up," Bob said.

"He already is. He said you were hungry," Jessica said.

"I should have stopped on the way," Bob mused. "But Ryan said he wanted to cook dinner."

"He loves cooking for people," Jessica replied.

"He's good at it," Bob said. "So how are you?" Kelsey stood and offered Jessica her seat. Jessica took the seat, and Kelsey handed Jessica the bowl of cheese puffs.

"I'm good," Jessica replied.

"Looking forward to working for me this summer?"

"Very much," Jessica replied as Kelsey took off her shoes and walked into the smaller of the two tents. Tyler was unrolling a sleeping bag.

"Need any help?" Kelsey asked Tyler. Tyler looked up from his kneeling position.

"I think I have it under control."

"You seem to," Kelsey said. She sat on the other unrolled sleeping bag and looked around the cozy tent.

"When are Morgan and Jasmine coming?" Tyler asked.

"When Morgan gets off work," Kelsey replied. "It should be soon." Tyler finished straightening the sleeping bag and placed a pillow at the top. He lay back on the sleeping bag.

"I always thought tents were small and uncomfortable," he said.

"Well, this is a four-person tent. You get more room, but it will be a little colder tonight. That's the trade-off."

"I see," Tyler said. He sat up, leaned over to Kelsey and kissed her.

"Thanks for inviting me," he said.

"I'm glad you could come," Kelsey replied.

A while later, Kelsey and Tyler were putting dishes on the wooden picnic table. Jessica had returned to the RV to help Ryan bring out dishes and Bob was sitting in the camp chair, working. Suddenly a silver Honda drove up and parked near the tent.

Kelsey ran over to the car, as Morgan and Jasmine got out.

"You're here!" Kelsey said happily, giving them both hugs.

"North!" Jasmine said in delight.

"Hey, Kels," Morgan said, excitedly. She looked around the campsite. "What is that?" she asked, looking at the giant RV.

"Ryan's Dad's RV. Come on, I'll introduce you," she said. The girls walked over to the campsite.

"Hi, Tyler," Jasmine and Morgan said together. They giggled.

"Hi," Tyler said, putting a rock on top of a stack of napkins so they wouldn't blow away. Kelsey led them to Bob, who was reading a memo.

"Bob?" Kelsey said. "Sorry to interrupt, these are my friends, Jasmine and Morgan." Bob looked up. To Kelsey's surprise, he closed the folder he was looking at and stood up. He tossed the folder in the chair.

"I'm Jasmine," Jazz said, sticking out her hand. Bob shook it.

"Hi, Jasmine. So you must be Morgan?" he said to Morgan, offering his hand to her.

Morgan shook his hand. "I am," she replied, smiling at him. Bob released her hand and looked at Kelsey.

"Kelsey, please go find out if Ryan's ready yet. It's time for dinner," Bob said.

"I'm starving," Morgan said.

"You just ate," Jasmine said. She glanced at Kelsey. "Morgan made me stop for donuts on the way here."

"I hope you brought extra," Kelsey said.

"Of course," Jasmine said. "I'll go with you. I want to say hi," she said. Kelsey and Jasmine walked into the RV. Kelsey hadn't been inside yet, having been enjoying the fresh air and time with Bob and Tyler. So she was shocked as they walked up the stairs.

"Wow," Jasmine said, as they walked into the RV.

Kelsey looked around. She had never been in an RV like this one. Stepping into was like stepping into a long luxury suite. She and Jasmine walked through the living room, which had seating for seven. Ryan and Jessica had taken over the dining nook, and it was covered with dishes of Brazilian food.

"Hi, Jazz," Ryan said as they walked to the gourmet kitchen. Ryan was right, there was plenty of room to cook.

"Hi, Ryan," Jasmine said.

"Where's Jess?" Kelsey asked, looking around.

"In the bedroom," Ryan said. "She wanted to freshen up." Kelsey glanced down the RV, and noted that she was still at least several feet from the door of the bedroom. The door opened and Jess walked out. Her hair was in a ponytail, and she had put on her extra fleece.

"Hey, Jasmine," she said, walking out and giving Jasmine a hug.

"Give them a tour, Jess. I'm almost done," Ryan said.

"Good, because Bob's about to die of hunger," Kelsey said to him.

"He sent you in?" Ryan asked.

"Yes."

"What a drama king. I'll be done in a minute," Ryan commented.

"Come on, let's look around," Jasmine said, pulling Kelsey. They followed Jessica into the bedroom, which was enormous, and had a beautiful bathroom attached. The decor of the RV was sleek masculine browns and beiges and looked like a well appointed and opulent hotel room.

"This is nicer than my house," Jasmine said.

"No kidding. And your house is really nice," Kelsey said.

"This is what camping should be," Jessica said. "Do you really expect us to sleep out in those fabric things outside?"

"We call them tents," Kelsey said.

"What if it rains?" Jessica said.

"It's fun," Jasmine said.

"Says you," Jessica said.

The girls walked around the bedroom, flipping the switch to raise the built-in television, and opening the huge closet. Then they walked back out into the kitchen, where Tyler had joined Ryan.

"It's done," Ryan said.

"Grab a dish," Jessica said. The five of them all took dishes, and began to carry them out of the RV. Bob and Morgan were sitting at the picnic table, chatting. Bob's paperwork was still sitting in the camp chair, his smartphone weighing it down from the wind.

"Finally," Bob said, as Ryan placed a dish of shrimp onto the table.

"It's worth the wait," Ryan countered.

"I don't doubt that," Bob replied. "Thanks for cooking." Ryan grinned.

"It's my pleasure," he said.

When all the dishes were on the table, they sat down to a Brazilian feast as dusk began to fall. As Kelsey expected, Bob didn't touch the spiced greens, but he didn't hesitate to try everything else that Ryan had prepared.

"The greens are really good, Dad," Ryan commented.

"Right," Bob said doubtfully.

"They are," Ryan pouted.

"Morgan isn't eating them," Bob pointed out.

Morgan wrinkled her nose. "I don't like vegetables much."

"You should try them," Kelsey said. "They're delicious."

"Maybe," Morgan said, doubtfully. "I'll try them if Bob does."

"We'll suffer together?" Bob said in amusement.

"Yes," Morgan said. She put a spoonful of the greens on his plate, then one on her own.

"Here goes," Bob said, taking a bite. Morgan did the same, Ryan looking at their faces in interest.

"Not bad. I prefer the shrimp though," Bob said. "What do you think, Morgan?"

"It's okay," she said.

"How can anyone not like vegetables?" Ryan asked.

"More for us," Tyler said, taking more of the greens.

"I guess that's what happens when you grow up in the Midwest. Land of meat," Ryan said.

"Lisa's from the Midwest. She eats vegetables," Tyler said.

"Where are you from, Bob?" Morgan asked, eating her rice and beans.

"Chicago," Bob replied, looking at her.

"Really? I've always wanted to go there," Morgan said.

"You've always wanted to go everywhere," Jasmine said.

"That's because I haven't been anywhere," Morgan retorted.

"Where have you been?" Jessica asked.

"Portland and Seattle," Morgan replied. "That's it."

"Not even Canada?" Tyler asked.

Morgan shook her head. "I don't have a passport," she said.

"You could get one of those special driver's licenses. That would substitute for a passport at the Canadian border," Tyler said.

"I should," Morgan replied.

"If you could go anywhere, where would you go?" Bob asked Morgan.

"Spain," Morgan replied. "It sounds so romantic."

"How about in the United States?" Bob asked.

"Los Angeles," Morgan said.

"Not New York?" Tyler asked.

"I saw Kels' pictures. I'd love to go, but I mean, come on, L.A.? All the celebrities, the beaches, Hollywood. I couldn't pass that up," Morgan replied.

"How about you, Jasmine? Have you traveled?" Bob asked her.

"We go on a trip every year," Jasmine said.

"Jasmine's been everywhere. She even has a passport," Kelsey said.

"You should get one," Tyler said to Kelsey. "That way we can go up to Vancouver and stay in Bob's condo before Ryan ruins it."

"Hey!" Ryan said. Bob laughed.

After an amazing dinner, Ryan and Tyler cleaned up while the girls sat with Bob at the table. Morgan had left to go to the bathroom.

"So now what do we do?" Jessica asked. Night had begun to fall.

"This," Kelsey said.

"Sit?" Jessica said.

"Talk. Eat dessert. Walk over to the beach. Be with each other," Kelsey replied.

"Seriously?" Jessica said.

"You're really a city person," Bob commented.

"I am," Jessica agreed.

"Ryan's the same. That's why I liked to drag him out here," Bob said.

"How often do you come here, Bob?" Jasmine asked.

"Ryan and I used to come every year when he was younger. But I haven't been here in years," Bob mused. "I've missed it."

"You should come more often," Kelsey said.

"I should," Bob replied. He looked up as Morgan left the RV and sat down at the table.

"That is the most amazing RV I've ever seen, Bob," she said.

"You like it?" Bob said.

"It's incredible," Morgan said.

Jessica yawned and Bob stood up.

"All right, ladies, it's back to work for me."

"You aren't having dessert?" Morgan asked him.

Bob smiled at her. "Not tonight. I'll see all of you in the morning."

"Good night," Morgan said, and the other girls said their goodbyes as Bob took his paperwork out of the camp chair and went back into the RV.

"Is he really going to work?" Morgan asked Kelsey.

"Probably."

"I can't believe he runs a company. He's so nice," Morgan said.

"I know," Jasmine said. "I'm not surprised he's nice though. So's Ryan."

"Yeah," Morgan said thoughtfully. Ryan and Tyler came out of the RV and sat at the table.

"Are you telling ghost stories yet?" Ryan asked.

"Not yet," Kelsey replied.

"Not ever," Jessica said. "Not if you want me to sleep."

They sat at the table for a while, talking about school and work. After a while, Tyler went into the RV and got dessert, which they ate at the table.

"Should we make a fire?" Ryan asked, feeding Jessica a spoonful of tiramisu.

"Not tonight. Tomorrow," Kelsey said. "I'm tired."

"Me too. It's been a long day," Morgan said, twisting her hair.

"I can't believe the beach is right there and we haven't walked on it," Tyler said, looking at the sparkling water that separated Fort Flagler from the Port Townsend waterfront.

"Let's go before bed," Kelsey said to him.

"Then let's go now," Jessica said, standing. "I don't know why I'm exhausted."

"It's the fresh air," Tyler said. Ryan covered the tiramisu, and the group headed across the parking lot to the beach that surrounded the campground. Ryan and Jessica stopped on the playground and the other four walked to the beach. Kelsey took Tyler's hand and he smiled at her.

"Aw, aren't you cute," Morgan said sarcastically.

"Don't be a hater, Morgan," Kelsey replied. "It will be your turn soon."

"No one's going out with me, Kels and you know it," Morgan said. "Unless I move out of Port Townsend."

"Don't be silly," Jasmine said.

"You know it's true," Morgan said, tossing her highlighted hair. "Just because they don't say that I'm trash, doesn't mean that no one thinks it."

"Morgan, you're awesome," Kelsey said.

"Yeah, tell that to the guys around here," Morgan said.

"Forget them. Who'd want to go out with them anyway?" Jasmine said.

Morgan sighed. "Maybe I'll move to Port Angeles," she said. "That's the only Angeles I'm likely to get to anytime soon."

"What's with you?" Kelsey asked her, as they walked on the sand.

"It's just been a bad week," Morgan said.

"Don't let it get to you," Kelsey said.

"I'll try. Tyler, do you know any billionaires looking for a girlfriend?"

"No, but tell Ryan to set you up. I'm sure he knows a few. They might only be millionaires, though."

"I'd be willing to settle," Morgan teased.

"Seriously, you're gorgeous. You'll find someone nice," Jasmine said.

"Maybe," Morgan said. "Ignore me. Let's enjoy the night."

"It's beautiful," Kelsey said. "Tyler, do you see the lights there?"

"That's Port Townsend?"

"It is."

"Wow, it seems so close," Tyler said, looking at the sparkling lights across the water.

"We aren't far," Kelsey replied.

"It feels like we're a world away," Tyler said, squeezing her hand.

Once their walk on the beach was over, they rejoined Ryan and Jessica, who had been sitting on a bench in the playground, holding hands. Everyone walked carefully back to the campsite and gathered their toiletries. Then, Kelsey leading the way back with a flashlight, they walked over to the campground bathroom to get ready for bed.

Kelsey, who had finished in the bathroom first, walked out to find Tyler standing against the wall, looking at his smartphone.

"Tsk," she said. "Can't get away from the internet," she taunted.

"Sorry, Miss North," Tyler said. He put the smartphone into his pocket and leaned over and kissed her.

"I'm taking away your camping badge," she said.

"Don't do that. Otherwise, I'll have to throw rocks at your tent at 3 a.m."

Kelsey laughed. "Jess and I will sleep right through it. Morgan, on the other hand, will come out and beat you up."

"Will guys seriously not date her?" Tyler asked Kelsey.

"People judge her by the trailer park she lives in and who her father is. Morgan and her sisters have developed a reputation for being rough around the edges."

"So?"

"Guys want nice girls like Jasmine," Kelsey said.

"And like you," Tyler added.

"I'm not a nice girl."

"I think you're very nice," Tyler said.

"Do you?" Kelsey said flirtily.

"Very," Tyler said, kissing her.

"Cut it out. Can't you keep your hands off of her?" Ryan said to Tyler as Ryan left the bathroom.

"No," Tyler said.

"And you complain about me and Jess."

"That's because you're annoying everywhere. Kelsey and I were alone, before you showed up," Tyler said.

"Are you guys fighting again?" Jessica asked as she, Jasmine, and Morgan left the bathroom.

"Always," Tyler said.

"Let's go," Kelsey said, turning on the flashlight. The group walked back to the campsite.

"Come on, Jess," Ryan said, once they arrived at the tents.

"I don't think so," Jessica said.

"We have separate tents for boys and girls, Ryan," Kelsey said.

"What? We're in sleeping bags. I have to sleep next to Tyler?" Ryan said.

"Lucky me," Tyler said, sarcastically.

"Seriously, Jess?" Ryan said.

"Goodnight, Ryan," Jessica said, and she walked into the girls' tent. Morgan and Jasmine followed her inside.

Ryan sighed and went into the boys' tent. Tyler wrapped his arms around Kelsey's waist.

"You can't keep your hands off of me, Mr. Olsen?" Kelsey teased.

"No, I can't," Tyler replied, kissing her.

The next morning, Kelsey sat up in her sleeping bag and stretched gently. She had slept comfortably, even though the air was chilly. She glanced over at the other three girls.

Jasmine had her arms wrapped around a teddy bear she had brought with her. Morgan slept with her hair in two braids, each tied with a pink ribbon, which framed her face and made her look adorable.

And Jessica was wearing a wool hat. Every part of her body, except for her face, was completely covered with blankets, the sleeping bag, and as Kelsey knew, two fleece jackets, sweatpants, and thick socks.

Kelsey quietly climbed out of her sleeping bag, put her shoes on at the door and left the tent. She zipped the flap back quickly so the cold morning air wouldn't wake the others.

She decided that it was cold enough to warrant making a fire, so she located the matches and the kindling and started one. She knelt next to the fire as it began, and warmed her hands. It was cold enough to see her breath, but she figured that it would warm up later. She looked at her phone. It was 8 a.m.

"Good morning," said a quiet voice behind Kelsey. She turned around and saw Tyler, who had just got out of his tent.

Her heart stopped as she looked at him in his just-out-of-bed hotness. He was wearing sweatpants and a Darrow Law Sweatshirt, but in Kelsey's view, he couldn't look better.

She hadn't seen him like this since she had stopped waking him up for fit month in October, but here Tyler was, supremely sexy. Kelsey bit her lip. Then she realized something. She was now his girlfriend.

She walked up to him and kissed him on the lips. Then, as she had wanted to do for months, she reached up and rumpled his hair with her hands. Tyler smiled at her sleepily.

"Good morning, Tyler," Kelsey said brightly.

"I'm going to get dressed," he said.

"You do that," Kelsey said, turning away from him. She was feeling as she always did when she saw him like this, warm and flushed, and like she should have a very cold shower. So much for needing the fire.

Over the next hour, Morgan, Jasmine, and Jess woke up and left the tent. Tyler sat in a camp chair, reading a book on his iPad as Jasmine went to the car to get the donuts that they had brought.

"Where's Ryan?" Jessica asked Tyler as Jasmine returned.

"He slept in the RV. He said he was cold," Tyler replied.

"Are you kidding me?" Kelsey said.

Morgan laughed. "City boy," she said.

"Tyler managed," Jasmine said.

"Tyler's not a wimp," Kelsey said.

"It was cold last night. Maybe I'll sleep in the RV," Jessica said.

"Then you will be sleeping next to Ryan. There's only two beds," Tyler commented.

"Really?" Jessica groused.

"How could you have possibly been cold in all of those layers?" Morgan asked. She twirled a braid with her finger.

"It was freezing," Jessica said. "It still is."

"It's part of the fun," Kelsey said.

"Right," Jessica said. "I'm going to sit by the fire. Scoot over, Tyler," she said, picking up a camp chair and moving it next to the fire, which was slowly dying.

"Do you think Ryan's up?" she asked him.

"I'll go check," Tyler said. He stood up, put his iPad on the table and walked over to the door of the RV. He punched in a code and walked in. He returned a few minutes later.

"Ryan's up. He's cooking breakfast," Tyler said, retrieving his iPad and sitting back down.

"Jazz and Morgan brought donuts for breakfast," Kelsey said.

"You can have them with your eggs benedict," Tyler replied.

Bob came out of the RV a while later, fully dressed in khakis and a navy fleece jacket. He was holding a stack of papers and his smartphone. He surveyed the group, who were all still in their sleepwear, and smiled. He sat at the table.

"Are you working again?" Morgan asked him.

Bob looked at her. "I work every day, Pippi," he said.

"Who?" Morgan asked.

"Pippi Longstocking. It's a children's book. The main character wore her hair like that. How old are you anyway?" Bob asked.

"Same age as Tyler," Kelsey offered.

"When's your birthday?" Morgan asked him.

"September 14th," Tyler said. "You?"

"September 2nd," Morgan replied.

"I thought you were the same grade as Kelsey," Jessica said.

"We moved to Port Townsend in first grade," Morgan said. "I had to redo the school year."

Bob laughed. "At least you didn't have to repeat it because of your grades," Bob said.

Kelsey looked at Bob in interest. "You did?"

"I didn't do very well in school," Bob offered.

"You're a lawyer," Jasmine said, in surprise.

"What do you call a law student who graduates with a D average?" Bob joked. "Attorney at Law. There's lots of lawyers who didn't do well in law school."

"I bet your mom did well," Kelsey said to Tyler.

"Not really," Tyler shrugged. "A little better than Ryan."

"Really?" Kelsey said.

"My mother says she partied her way through college. But she aced the LSAT. Her counselor told her she'd never get into the law schools she applied to. Lisa considers it a minor miracle that she made it through first year."

"So why are you working so hard?" Morgan asked Kelsey.

"I'm beginning to wonder. Maybe I'm hurting my chances of being a billionaire," Kelsey replied.

"It's good to work hard," Bob countered. "It makes you a better person."

"I guess I can look forward to that then," Morgan commented.

"Yeah, no one works harder than you," Jasmine said, patting her arm. "It will pay off."

"What do you do?" Bob asked Morgan.

"I work at the Maritime Center. I'm an administrative assistant."

"Hard work?" Bob asked in interest.

"I've been doing a lot of overtime. I'm saving to get my own place," Morgan replied.

"Good for you. You live at home?"

Morgan nodded, as Ryan opened the door of the RV.

"Breakfast time!" he said cheerfully.

"I've never eaten better camping food," Jasmine said, as she Kelsey and Morgan sat on the beach.

"I've never eaten better food," Morgan commented. "Ryan's an amazing chef."

"And he learned for Jessica. That's so sweet," Jasmine said.

"I wonder what we're having for lunch?" Kelsey mused.

"Lobster? With caviar?" Morgan guessed.

"Don't give Ryan any ideas," Kelsey said.

"Is he really going to spend the vacation cooking meals in the RV?" Jasmine asked.

"I think so. He doesn't like the cold."

"Neither does Jess," Morgan said. Jessica was also in the RV, watching television. Tyler was sitting in the camp chair back at the campsite, reading. Bob was sitting at the picnic table, working. He had been on a conference call when they left.

Kelsey shook her head. "This is some camping trip," she commented.

Jasmine giggled. "At least Tyler's having fun," she said.

"That's true," Kelsey said. Tyler did seem to be enjoying the quiet.

"Relax, North. Enjoy your time away from school," Jasmine said.

"I am. I can't believe we were at Darrow this time yesterday," Kelsey commented.

"It's nice to be here. And it's warming up," Jasmine said. Morgan dragged her finger through the sand.

"Do you want to go to the store?" Kelsey asked. "I'd love some coffee."

"I bet there's an espresso machine in that thing," Morgan said, referring to the RV.

"I bet there is. But I like the coffee at the store."

"You like the idea of the coffee at the store. It feels like you're really camping," Morgan said.

"Exactly."

"Let's go. Kelsey can pretend that she's roughing it," Jasmine said, standing.

The girls stopped by the campsite to see if anyone wanted anything. Bob was still on his conference call, but Tyler put his iPad in the tent and joined them. They walked around the RV, and Morgan stopped suddenly.

"Is this Bob's?" she asked. They were standing in front of a marine-blue Maserati, which had been parked behind the RV.

"Yes," Tyler said.

"He has a Maserati?" Morgan said. "Wow."

"It's pretty," Jasmine said, peering at the front.

They walked around the car, so Morgan could admire it. Then they walked out of the campsite, crossed the parking lot, and less than thirty seconds later, were standing on the deck outside of the store.

"Long trip," Tyler said.

"I told you there was a store a few yards away," Kelsey reminded him as they walked in.

The store was inside a little hut, and it held all of the necessities for a fun camping trip. Sunscreen, bandages, and toy buckets for the sand sat on the shelf. Kelsey ordered three lattes — one with hazelnut syrup — from the snack bar while the others looked around. Tyler walked up holding a kite.

"Let's get this," he said to her.

"Have you flown a kite before?" Kelsey asked, taking it from his hand and putting it on the counter. Tyler shook his head.

"This should be fun," Morgan commented. "What do I owe you, Kels?"

"My treat," Tyler said.

"Forget it," Kelsey said to him.

"Kelsey."

"Forget it, I said. This is my town," Kelsey said.

"You let me pay in New York," Tyler pointed out.

"You always pay. It's my turn," Kelsey said.

"Fine. You pay here, and I can buy you anything I want in Portland," Tyler countered.

"Nope," Kelsey said, taking out her wallet, and paying for the goods.

"That's what you think," Tyler said petulantly, taking his kite and leaving the store.

"Kelsey, he has two billion dollars," Morgan said.

"He doesn't need to spend it on me," Kelsey said, picking up a drink and handing it to Morgan. Morgan took her coffee cup, and Kelsey picked up the other two and followed Morgan outside. Tyler and Jasmine were sitting at one of the picnic tables on the deck and Jasmine was checking her email.

"Enjoying the free wi-fi?" Kelsey asked Jasmine.

"Very much," Jasmine said. Kelsey set Tyler's coffee in front of him.

"Thank you," he said.

"You're welcome," Kelsey smiled.

"We have a contract," Tyler said. "You get Port Townsend, I get Portland."

"Stop being annoying," Kelsey said and Tyler grinned.

"You haven't seen how annoying I can be," he said.

"Yeah, that's a threat," Kelsey commented. "I can imagine."

"Good. Then you'll behave," Tyler said. Kelsey rolled her eyes and took a sip of her coffee. It was pretty good. It certainly beat Darrow's dining hall swill.

"Thanks for the coffee, Kels," Morgan said.

"You're welcome. How's the hazelnut?" Kelsey asked.

"Good. Have a sip," Morgan said, handing Kelsey the cup. Kelsey had a taste of the coffee. The hazelnut syrup made it extra tasty. Kelsey handed the cup back to Morgan.

"So are we learning how to fly a kite today, Mr. Olsen?"

"Did we have other plans?" Tyler asked.

"I thought we could sit in the cold and look at each other for the rest of the day," Kelsey teased.

"Tempting," Tyler said. "But I bet we can fit kite flying into that busy schedule."

After they finished their coffee, they returned to the RV to invite the others to join them in kite flying. But Ryan and Jessica were curled up on the sofa watching a basketball game, and Bob was on another call. So Kelsey, Jasmine, Morgan, and Tyler headed to the beach without them.

"Am I allowed to assemble the kite, or is it like the tent, and purely for Miss North to make?" Tyler asked her.

"Funny. Perhaps you'd like to find a rock under your sleeping bag tonight?" Kelsey asked him.

"Two can play that game," Tyler warned her.

Tyler carefully read the instructions and made the red-and-blue kite, as the girls supervised and made suggestions.

"Are you having fun, Tyler?" Jasmine asked him a bit later as she, Kelsey, and Tyler sat on the beach and Morgan ran down the sand, taking her turn at flying the kite in the cold wind.

"This is amazing," Tyler said.

"You've been to Fort Flagler before," Kelsey said.

"Yeah, but we didn't do much, except sit in the RV and watch Bob work. The three of you know how to enjoy the outdoors."

"We'll have to go on a long walk tomorrow. Drag Jess and Ryan out into the wild," Kelsey said to him, as she watched the kite.

"That sounds great," Tyler said. He lay back on the cool ground and looked up at the sky.

"I'm glad you and Morgan could join us," Kelsey said to Jasmine.

"I know. I'll probably only see you one more time before I get married," Jasmine replied.

"Are you really going to make me wear hot pink?" Kelsey asked her.

"Is that really all you care about?" Jasmine asked.

"Yes. I know that Jim loves you, so I don't have to object to the marriage. I'm going to duck when you throw the bouquet, so I'm not worried about catching that either. What else is there to care about?"

"I guess you have a point," Jasmine said. "You don't want the bouquet? I think Morgan's been practicing her catching skills."

"She can have it. I'm not getting married anytime soon," Kelsey said.

Jasmine glanced at Tyler. "No comments from you, Tyler?"

"Nope. I don't want to get into trouble with Miss North," Tyler said.

"You don't want to get married soon, either," Kelsey pointed out.

"How do you know?" Tyler asked her.

"Stop teasing me, Tyler," Kelsey said.

Tyler grinned. "I'll get married when my bride wants to," he replied. Jasmine looked at Kelsey meaningfully, but Kelsey refused to react. Tyler was exasperating. Frankly, so was Jasmine.

"Don't think I didn't notice that you changed the subject, Jasmine Jefferson. What about my dress?" Kelsey said.

"You and Morgan will look great. We'll come to Seattle in May and pick out dresses."

"Super fun," Kelsey said sarcastically.

After a couple of hours of kite flying and sitting on the beach talking, they wandered back to the campsite for lunch. Ryan had messaged them that it was ready, and they arrived back to the campsite with the plates and three salads already on the table.

"Done working?" Morgan asked Bob as she sat next to him.

"For now," he replied, smiling at her.

"Why are you working so much?" Tyler asked Bob.

"Because I'm supposed to be in Seattle this week. Only your mother and Carol know I'm here," Bob replied.

"I see," Tyler laughed.

"What did you guys do?" Jessica asked, as she brought out a large basket of waffle fries and placed it on the table.

"Flew a kite," Kelsey said.

"For two hours?" Jessica asked.

"We sat around and talked too," Kelsey said.

"That's it?" Jessica said.

"That's what we do when we camp," Kelsey commented.

"I'm understanding why Bob brought work," Jessica said.

"Aren't you feeling relaxed, Jess?" Bob asked her.

"Not really. I keep wondering what's next," Jessica replied.

"I thought we'd go on a long walk tomorrow," Kelsey said.

"Not today?" Jessica asked.

"The day's half over. Let's go tomorrow," Kelsey said. "Anyway, Jazz and Morgan leave tonight."

"Back to work?" Bob asked Morgan.

"Yes. I'm not a billionaire, so I have to," she replied.

"Working hard is how I became a billionaire, Miss Morgan," Bob said. Morgan smiled at him.

Ryan walked out of the RV with a platter piled with sandwiches. "What did you make for lunch, Ryan?" Bob asked.

"Bob food. Sloppy Joes," Ryan said, putting the platter down on the table.

"Almost camping food. Yum," Kelsey said.

"I thought it would make my father happy," Ryan said.

"I'm a simple man, Ryan," Bob replied, He picked up his fork and lifted one of the sandwiches onto his plate. The others passed around the salads and side dishes that Ryan had made. Once everyone had filled their plates, they began eating.

"Delicious, Ryan," Jasmine said.

"Yeah, you can come camping with us any time," Morgan said. She wiped sauce off her lips with a napkin.

"It's fun, now that I have something to do," Ryan said, cutting into his Sloppy Joe with a knife.

"Maybe I should have brought my knitting," Jessica mused.

"Who's the type A one now? Relax, Miss Hunter," Kelsey said.

"Who can relax? It's so quiet, it makes me nervous," Jessica said.

"Spoken like a true New Yorker," Bob said.

"Everyone knows that you only have to worry when it's peaceful," Jessica said.

"I think you've seen too many movies, Jess," Kelsey said, eating a waffle fry. "Are you two coming back out while we're here?" she asked Morgan and Jasmine.

"You should. I have lots more to cook," Ryan said.

"I can't," Jasmine said. "It's still fit month at my house, but you should, Morgan."

"Great, I can keep cheating on my diet," Morgan said.

Jasmine scowled at her. "I'm weighing you when they leave," she said.

"No, you aren't," Morgan said. "When do you guys go?"

"Thursday morning," Kelsey replied.

"I'll come back, but it will have to be after work. I don't want you guys to have to eat in the dark, though."

"We'll save you a plate," Kelsey said.

"I'll message you," Morgan said, taking a forkful of cole slaw.

"You're certainly quiet, Tyler," Jessica said.

"Enjoying the moment, Miss Hunter," he replied. "I'll be frantic back in Seattle."

"You really should quit Law Review," Ryan said.

"I can't quit. I'll be editor next year," Tyler replied.

"You're not going to have any fun," Ryan said.

"Oh, I doubt that," Tyler said, looking at Kelsey. She blushed.

Everyone, including Bob, walked down to the beach after lunch and sat on the driftwood logs. Jessica zipped up her pink fleece jacket up to the neck, and sat next to Ryan, who was wearing a jacket over two sweaters. Tyler sat next to Kelsey and looked out over the water to Port Townsend. And Bob sat on a log with Jasmine and Morgan and checked his phone messages.

"Are you really Ryan's father?" Morgan asked him.

"I am," Bob replied. "Why?"

"You don't act like a parent," she replied.

"And how do parents act?" Bob asked her.

Morgan was thoughtful for a moment.

"Stressed out," she finally replied.

"Ryan doesn't stress me," Bob said.

"Are you kidding me?" Tyler said.

"He stresses you," Bob answered.

"It's because Tyler's always telling me what to do," Ryan said.

"Someone has to be responsible around here," Tyler replied.

"So I leave it up to you," Bob said to Tyler, who laughed.

"That's your secret of youth. Let Ryan give me the gray hairs," Tyler commented.

"You're like your mother," Bob said. "Busy taking responsibility for everything and everyone. Why shouldn't I let you? I let her." Bob put his phone in his pocket, and slid down the log and onto the coarse sand.

"Perhaps I should study your philosophy more closely," Tyler said to Bob.

"Maybe. You'd have more fun," Bob replied.

"Nah. Tyler would still worry about everything," Ryan said.

"Probably," Tyler agreed.

"This was a great idea, to come out here," Bob said, looking at the water.

"And we still have four nights left," Kelsey said. She leaned her head on Tyler's shoulder. He smiled at her.

"I won't survive," Jessica said.

"Of course you will. You just need a different mindset," Tyler replied.

"You aren't having fun, Jess?" Jasmine asked.

"I'm just not used to doing nothing," Jessica said.

"But that's the point of camping. To relax and enjoy nature," Kelsey said.

"Perhaps someone should have warned me about that," Jessica replied.

Jasmine and Morgan loaded their things into Morgan's car at dusk. Kelsey gave Jasmine a hug.

"Be kind about our bridesmaid dresses. Rethink the bright pink," Kelsey said to her.

Jasmine shook her black hair and giggled. "Never," she replied. Kelsey scowled.

Morgan shook Bob's hand. "It was nice to meet you," she said to him.

"I hope you'll come back for dinner while we're here," he replied.

"I will," Morgan said. "It's free food."

Bob laughed.

"See you," Tyler said to the girls.

"So you're coming to my wedding?" Jasmine asked him.

"I wouldn't miss it," Tyler replied. Jasmine beamed.

The girls got into the car. They had said their goodbyes to Ryan and Jessica earlier, so Ryan and Jess could return to the grocery store for fresh supplies. They put on their seat belts, and Morgan started the car. She beeped the horn and they drove off.

"That was fun," Tyler said to Kelsey, as they walked over to the picnic table.

"It was. Your friends are very nice," Bob said.

Tyler glanced at Bob. "You think so?" he asked him.

"Quiet, you," Bob replied with a smile. Tyler grinned.

A few minutes later, Ryan and Jessica pulled up, and hopped out of

Ryan's Porsche.

"Did you see Morgan?" Kelsey asked them as Ryan pulled a bag out of the back seat.

"We passed them on the way back," Ryan said. "Morgan drives faster than I do," he said, almost in admiration.

"She's a daredevil," Kelsey said, taking the bag from Ryan's hands. Tyler took the bag from her and walked it over to the picnic table. "Thanks, Tyler," she said.

"What's for dinner?" Bob asked Ryan.

"It's a surprise," Ryan replied.

"A good surprise or a bad one?" Bob retorted.

"You'll see," Ryan replied.

"I can drive to McDonald's," Bob said to him.

"Trust me, it will be better than that," Ryan said, taking out another bag.

An hour and a half later, the group sat down to spinach lasagna. It was beginning to get dark, so Kelsey had put a lantern on the table.

"Again with the green things," Bob said.

"You're eating it, aren't you?" Ryan replied.

"I waited ninety minutes for it, so now I have a lot of sunk costs," Bob retorted.

"It's good for you," Ryan said, unapologetically.

"What's with you and this healthy living stuff?" Bob asked. "Organic vegetables, meditation? You're turning into Lisa."

"I learned a lot when I was traveling in Asia," Ryan replied.

"That was money wasted then," Bob said. Ryan laughed.

After dinner, Bob, Jessica, and Ryan returned to the RV to watch another basketball game, while Kelsey and Tyler walked back to the beach facing Port Townsend.

"You seem very relaxed," Kelsey said to him. She sat on the sand, her back against a log, while Tyler's head rested on a pillow in Kelsey's lap. The pillow had been created out of one of his new flannel shirts. Kelsey ruffled his hair with her hand.

"I am," Tyler replied. "This is wonderful. We should buy a place out here."

Kelsey decided to ignore the 'we'. Although she loved him, Tyler was much more sure of their future together than she was. Despite everything they had been through, Kelsey couldn't bear to get her hopes up.

"Why hasn't Bob bought a place here? Why did he get the RV instead?" she asked.

"Bob bought the RV after he divorced wife number two. He decided that he and Ryan needed some male bonding time. He used it for about a year and a half. Then he married wife number three, and she and her four daughters descended on Medina. So that was the end of male bonding. By the time Bob divorced her, Ryan was too old to be interested in coming out here. It's basically been in mothballs since," Tyler replied.

"It's nice. It's like a palace," Kelsey said.

"I guess," Tyler replied. "I'm enjoying the tent."

"Are you really? You aren't too cold?" Kelsey knew that her tent would be colder without the body heat of Jasmine and Morgan tonight.

"It's perfect," Tyler replied. "No Ryan."

"I'm sorry Jess isn't having a good time," she said.

"She'll like Portland," Tyler said. "We all will. It's a short trip. I'm surprised you haven't made it back there."

"Too busy here," Kelsey said.

"Doing my bidding last summer."

"Spending time with you," Kelsey gently corrected him.

"I'm so lucky to have found you," Tyler said.

"I'm glad you think so," Kelsey said, leaning down and kissing him.

The next morning after breakfast, Kelsey, Tyler, Ryan, and Jessica packed a backpack full of snacks and water before they set off on a hike.

"How long will we be gone?" Jessica said, putting her hat on over her auburn curls.

"A couple hours," Kelsey said.

"That long?" Jessica asked doubtfully.

"We'll have fun. We're just going to visit the park. There's a lot to see."

"I bet," Jessica said doubtfully. Around his neck, Ryan knotted the scarf that Jessica had made for him.

"We can hold hands," Ryan said.

Jessica smiled at him. "We could do that here. In the RV."

"Nature is good for you Miss Hunter," Tyler commented.

"Hmm," Jessica said. Tyler put the backpack on his back.

"Not too heavy?" Kelsey asked him in concern.

"It's fine," Tyler replied. "Let's go," he said brightly.

They walked across the campground and up to one of the many walking trails that crossed Fort Flagler, leaving Bob behind. It was Monday, so Bob had a full day of work ahead of him, particularly since everyone at Tactec, save Lisa and Carol, thought he was sitting in his office.

Kelsey led them into the woods, and the ground felt hard under their feet. Tyler looked at all of the trees and plants around them in interest, while Jessica and Ryan walked behind him, holding hands. Jessica looked scared.

"It's dark," she commented.

"The trees are throwing shadows. We're fine," Kelsey said.

"Are you sure there are no bears?" Jessica asked.

"Positive," Kelsey replied.

Ryan squeezed Jessica's shoulders. "I'll keep you safe," he said.

"How? Let the bear eat you first?" Jessica snapped.

Tyler suppressed a laugh behind Kelsey.

Kelsey led them off the trail and over to the bunkers that Tyler had seen on the drive into the campground.

"These are awesome," Tyler said, as they walked through the large concrete structures.

"It's weird to think that this used to be an actual military base," Jessica said, looking around.

"Part of the 'triangle of fire' to protect Puget Sound," Kelsey commented.

"Why? Who would want to invade Seattle?" Ryan asked.

"Oh, I don't know, Ryan. There's only Boeing making defense planes, the Everett Shipyards, and also several million people. Did you sleep through history class?" Tyler asked him.

"No," Ryan pouted.

"The soldiers must have been bored to death," Jessica commented, putting her hand on the cold concrete wall.

"I imagine they had things to do," Kelsey said wryly. "I don't think there's a lot of downtime in the military."

"I guess," Jessica said.

After their visit to the bunkers, Kelsey led them back onto the trail. Tyler took her hand as they walked among the tall pine trees. Ryan looked at the ground in interest.

"Kelsey, do you think that you can find fiddlehead ferns here?" he asked her.

"Sure. Why?"

"I've been reading about foraging. It seems to be the next thing in cooking," Ryan said.

"I wouldn't do any foraging here. It's a state park," Kelsey replied.

"I know, I was just curious," Ryan said.

"I'm not eating anything you've picked off the ground," Jessica warned him.

"Where do you think vegetables come from?" Tyler asked her.

"The grocery store," Jessica replied sassily.

"Right," Tyler said to her. "We should take Jess blueberry picking this summer," he said to Kelsey.

"We should. It's so much fun, Jess," Ryan said.

"I bet," Jessica said doubtfully.

They continued down the path. Tyler breathed deeply and put his arm around Kelsey's shoulder.

"Thank you for bringing me here," he said quietly.

"You're welcome," Kelsey replied.

"What was that?" Jessica shouted. Kelsey and Tyler turned around.

"What?" Kelsey asked. Jessica was ashen, and was pointing at the base of a shrub that sat next to the trail.

"That!" Jessica said. Kelsey got closer to the shrub and knelt down.

"Be careful, Kels," Ryan said as he and Jessica moved farther away. Kelsey lifted a branch of the shrub, and as fast as lightning, a tiny garden snake fled and zipped across the trail in front of Jessica.

"A snake!" Jessica screamed.

Kelsey stood up. "It's just a garden snake. It won't hurt you," she said, rubbing her hands on the front of her jeans.

"There are snakes out here?" Jessica asked in dismay.

"None of them are poisonous. Western Washington doesn't have any poisonous ones," Kelsey said.

"So a snake couldn't come over from Eastern Washington?" Jessica said.

"Unlikely. Anyway, it would be a rattler. We'd hear him," Kelsey said

"You aren't helping," Tyler whispered to her.

"OMG. I cannot believe there are snakes here and you didn't tell me!" Jessica said.

"Jess, we're in the wilderness. That's where they live," Kelsey said patiently.

"I'm going back to the RV," Jessica said.

"What?" Kelsey said.

"I can't deal with snakes," Jessica said.

"I'll go back with you, Jess," Ryan said soothingly.

"Seriously?" Kelsey said.

"I'm sleeping in the RV tonight," Jessica said. "No way am I sleeping outside with snakes."

Kelsey sighed. "Fine," she said in resignation. "We'll walk you guys back."

After Kelsey and Tyler walked Jessica and Ryan back to the RV, where Bob was in the middle of his fifth conference call of the day, they returned to the trail. Tyler kissed Kelsey's hand.

"At least we'll have some quiet time," he said.

"I can't believe Jessica is such a wimp," Kelsey groused.

"She's just not used to the outdoors," Tyler said.

"I guess that's true. She could certainly face down anyone on the New York subway," Kelsey said thoughtfully.

"Different skill sets," Tyler agreed.

"I'll forgive her then. I'm not sure how she's going to cope with the next three nights, though."

"You heard her. She's sleeping in the RV," Tyler said. "I guess I'm getting Ryan back."

"Sorry," Kelsey giggled.

"It's okay. He can have the warm blanket," Tyler said.

"We have Jasmine and Morgan's sleeping bags too. That should keep him warm enough," Kelsey said.

"Otherwise, I guess he can sleep on the floor of the RV," Tyler mused.

"If Jess will let him. She still doesn't trust Ryan to keep his hands to himself."

"She's so cute. Ryan's not going to touch Jess without a notarized permission slip," Tyler commented. "He's not going to risk losing her."

Kelsey leaned her head on Tyler's arm and he kissed her hair as they walked slowly through the woods.

"At least you're having a good time," she said.

"This has been incredible," Tyler said.

"I'm glad," Kelsey replied. "It's nice to be able to share this with you."

"Is this where your family usually camped?" Tyler asked.

"No, we only came here occasionally. It doesn't feel like a vacation, since it's so easy to get home. We used to go to Kalaloch."

"'Clay-Lock'?" Tyler pronounced it. "How do you spell that?"

"K-a-l-a-l-o-c-h," Kelsey replied. "It's south of Forks, on the Pacific Ocean. About a three-hour drive away."

"Nice," Tyler said.

"I shouldn't be too hard on Jess, though," Kelsey smiled. "There's a guest lodge there, and we usually ate lunch at the restaurant there instead of cooking."

"That's cheating," Tyler commented with a grin.

"Did I mention the superstore in Forks, with the premium grocery store? That was a must-visit on any trip," Kelsey added.

"I'm telling," Tyler said. "I thought you were roughing it."

"I didn't say I was roughing it without Reese's peanut butter cups and soft ice cream. They had that at the campground too," Kelsey said.

"So much for being a nature girl," Tyler said.

They walked through the forest, eventually making their way to a quiet clearing, where they sat and had their snacks.

"You aren't afraid of snakes?" Kelsey teased.

"No," Tyler said, pulling out a bottle of water and handing it to her.

"Bears?"

"Not today."

"Then what are you afraid of?"

"You," Tyler said, opening a bottle of water of his own.

"Me? Why?" Kelsey asked in surprise.

"You have my heart in your hands," he said, taking a drink.

Kelsey smiled at him. "When did you become so poetic?" she asked.

"When I saw you," Tyler replied.

Tyler and Kelsey stayed out on the numerous trails for hours, holding hands, mostly walking in silence. They walked through the dense forest, replete with tall trees and big green ferns. They breathed in the fresh, damp air.

Eventually, they decided to walk back to camp. When they arrived, the campsite was quiet, and the Porsche was gone. Kelsey sat at the picnic table, while Tyler went into the RV. He returned a few minutes later.

"Ryan and Jess went to the grocery store, and Bob's on a call with my mother," he reported.

"Has anyone figured out that he's not in Seattle?" Kelsey asked, as Tyler sat down and picked up a granola bar.

"Not yet. Carol has an iron lock on the door to Bob's office, so no one's likely to find out," he said. "Are you hungry? Ryan baked chocolate chip muffins."

"Really? Margaret's recipe?" Kelsey asked. She loved Margaret's chocolate chip muffins.

"Probably, but I didn't taste them. Hold on, I'll get you one," Tyler walked back to the RV, and returned with a muffin for Kelsey. She bit into it happily. It was as good as Margaret's.

"Bob's off the phone. He'll be out in a minute," Tyler said, sitting at the picnic table with her.

"Thanks for this," Kelsey said.

"Sure," Tyler said. Bob walked out of the RV and sat down next to Kelsey.

"Did you have a nice walk in the woods?" Bob asked.

"It was good," Kelsey said, between bites.

"I think Jessica's going to have nightmares tonight," Bob commented.

"I feel bad. I didn't realize she was afraid of snakes."

"Why would you? It's not like there's a bunch of them on campus," Tyler said.

"She'll get over it," Bob said. "How's the muffin?"

"Great? Do you want a bite?" Kelsey said, holding the muffin out. Bob shook his head no.

"Are you done yet?" Tyler asked Bob.

"I have another call at six," Bob said.

"Have you been outside at all?" Kelsey asked him.

"I took my calls outside when Ryan and Jess were cooking. It's a nice day."

"A little cold," Kelsey said.

"I'm from Chicago. This is shorts-wearing weather," Bob replied.

"You sound like my mom," Tyler said.

"I've never been anywhere as cold as Minneapolis. I'd rather stand naked next to Lake Michigan in the dead of winter than go back to Minnesota in January," Bob commented.

"Have you been to Minneapolis?" Kelsey asked Tyler.

"Yes, but not lately. My grandmother prefers to come here."

"So she can meddle in Lisa's private life," Bob commented.

Tyler grinned. "Yeah, she's good at that."

"Does she know about Mayer?" Bob asked Tyler.

"That's a good question. I don't think so, unless she's read about him in the media. Otherwise, she probably would have come to Seattle to meet him," Tyler replied.

"Your poor mother," Bob said, smiling.

Kelsey finished the muffin as Ryan's Porsche roared back into the campsite. Ryan and Jessica got out, and Ryan began hauling bags out of the back seat.

"What's for dinner?" Bob asked Ryan as Ryan put a bag on the picnic table.

"A surprise," Ryan said petulantly.

"Are green vegetables involved?" Bob asked.

"Maybe," Ryan replied.

"Then I'm driving into town. Does anyone want anything?" Bob said, looking at Ryan.

"I'm making *varenyky*." Ryan admitted.

"You aren't really. How do you know how to make *varenyky*?" Bob challenged him.

"What's *varenyky*?" Jessica asked.

"Ukrainian dumplings," Bob said.

"I thought you were Russian," Jessica said.

"Ukraine was part of Russia when our family left," Ryan said.

"We're Ukrainian," Bob said to Jessica. "Are you really making *varenyky*?" Bob asked Ryan.

"It was supposed to be a surprise," Ryan said.

"I don't believe you can make them," Bob said.

"I can too," Ryan said. "They're delicious."

Bob surveyed him. "All right. We'll see. I've eaten a lot of *varenyky*," Bob said.

"These will be the best you ever had," Ryan said.

"No. That won't be possible," Bob replied. "But you're welcome to try."

"That sounds like a dare," Ryan said.

"Ryan, I grew up down the street from St. Nicholas. I ate *varenyky* from all of the babas in the neighborhood."

"Babas?" Jess asked.

"Old ladies," Bob said. "Do you really think you can make *varenyky* better than my grandmother?"

Ryan thought for a moment. "Yes," he finally said.

"Fine. Your *varenyky* is better than anyone else's and I'll double your allowance for the month," Bob said.

"If not?" Tyler asked.

Ryan thought for a minute. "I'll give you the keys to my Porsche for a month, after we get back from Portland."

"You're confident," Bob said in surprise.

"I am," Ryan replied.

"Good luck. I'm going to be honest with you," Bob said.

"Okay," Ryan said. He picked up the bag and went into the RV. Tyler followed him carrying another bag.

"I hope you're looking forward to hanging around campus for a month," Bob said to Jessica.

"I have faith in Ryan," she replied.

"Ryan's never had real *varenyky*," Bob said. "He won't know how to make them taste good."

Ryan returned from the RV. "Kels, is Morgan coming out tonight?" he asked.

"She messaged me that she'll return tomorrow. She's got to work late tonight," Kelsey said.

"Okay," Ryan said, taking the last bag and returning to the RV.

"So did you guys have fun?" Jessica asked Kelsey.

"We did."

"Sorry for being such a whiner," Jessica said.

"It's okay. I was busy bad-mouthing you, but I wouldn't know what to do if someone tried pick my pocket," Kelsey replied.

"We don't put things in pockets in New York," Jessica replied.

"Exactly. Are you going to sleep in the RV tonight?"

"No. Ryan said he'd give me the bed, but I decided I was overreacting. Also, there are no holes in the tent big enough for a snake, right?"

"It's hole-free," Kelsey said soothingly.

A half hour later, Ryan and Tyler brought out the first of the *varenyky*.

"That was quick," Bob said, looking up from his smartphone. He had been talking to the girls when a message from work had come in.

"You have a call at 6. Anyway, I had done a lot of the prep work earlier," Ryan said.

"You sure you want to give up your car? I'll let you out of our bet," Bob said.

"I'm sure," Ryan said. "Try them."

"Sour cream?" Bob asked.

"Here," Ryan said, placing a small dish next to Bob. Tyler placed a plate of dumplings in front of Jessica and one in front of Kelsey.

"What's this on top?" Jessica asked.

"Fried *salo*." Ryan replied.

"*Salo*? Where did you get salo around here?" Bob asked.

"It was in the fridge. I asked for it to be brought along," Ryan replied.

"We had *salo* and I didn't know?" Bob said.

"And what is *salo*?" Jessica asked.

"Pork fat. What pasta is to Italians, *salo* is to Ukrainians," Bob said. "All right, here goes nothing." Bob put his fork into the sour cream, then into one of the dumplings. He picked it up with his fork and took a large bite. Ryan looked at him expectantly, as did Kelsey, Tyler and Jessica.

Bob chewed slowly. He looked at Ryan.

"Well," he said.

"Well?" Ryan asked.

"We'll call it a draw," Bob said.

"Really? I thought I was going to lose my car," Ryan said. Jessica laughed.

"No, these are really good. I'm shocked. Where did you get the recipe?"

"Online. Someone said it was their grandmother's," Ryan said.

"You've made them before?" Bob asked.

"A couple of times. I tested them on Tyler," Ryan replied.

"You tested them on a Norwegian? What does Tyler know about *varenyky*?"

"I know what I like," Tyler said. Bob smiled at him and Ryan stood.

"I'm going to get some for myself," Ryan said.

"Eat lightly. I want more," Bob said. Ryan grinned and went into the RV as Kelsey and Jessica tucked into their food. The *varenyky* were delicious. Ryan returned with plates for himself and Tyler.

"Thanks," Tyler said, as Ryan placed a plate and fork in front of him. Bob took another large forkful of sour cream and ate another dumpling.

"Does your mother have any favorite Norwegian dishes?" Kelsey asked Tyler.

"My mother was raised on Froot Loops and Twinkies," Tyler replied. "So no."

"These are really great, Ryan," Jessica said. "I like the *salo*."

"If I hadn't eaten a muffin, I'd want seconds," Kelsey said.

"How was the muffin?" Ryan asked her.

"Delicious," she said.

Bob finished his first plate of *varenyky*, then began a second. He looked at his phone.

"I have to go. Nobody touch my *varenyky*," Bob said, rising.

"Do you want to put it inside? It's going to get cold," Ryan said.

"Nope. It will get me off the phone faster. Otherwise, you can fry them for me," Bob replied. He went into the RV.

"Okay, I'm full," Kelsey said, leaning against Tyler.

"Those were really good," Tyler said.

"I'm so glad I didn't lose my car," Ryan replied.

Later that night, after Bob finished the *varenyky* and Tyler, Jessica, and Ryan had eaten dessert, Kelsey and Tyler sat on the beach together holding hands.

"Nice day?" Kelsey asked.

"Always with you," Tyler replied.

The next day, Ryan and Jessica drove to Port Townsend for the day. Tyler and Kelsey went for another walk, this time out to Marrowstone Point. When they returned late in the day, they walked into the campsite to find Morgan and Bob, sitting at the picnic table talking.

"Hey, babe," Morgan said, as Kelsey sat next to her and gave her a hug.

"Hey, yourself. How long have you been here?"

"Only about twenty minutes. I got off on time today," Morgan replied.

"I don't think we have dinner yet?" Tyler asked Bob.

"Ryan and Jess aren't back yet," Bob said. "I think we're getting take-out."

"Ryan's not cooking?" Kelsey said in surprise.

"I think Ryan's resting on his laurels," Bob said. "He's still pretty proud of last night's dinner. I've got to admit, he did good."

"What did you have?" Morgan asked.

"Dumplings. They were fantastic," Kelsey replied.

"Can you cook?" Bob asked Morgan.

Morgan giggled. "No," she said.

"You can too. Morgan's an awesome cook," Kelsey said. "Stop being modest."

"I can't cook as well as Ryan," Morgan said.

"Ryan's spent the last year perfecting his skills," Tyler said.

"Where are Ryan and Jessica?" Morgan asked.

"In town. You probably drove past them," Kelsey said.

"Could be. I just wanted to get out of there," Morgan replied.

"Long day?" Bob asked.

"Probably not as long as your day usually is," Morgan said.

"That's probably true," Bob replied. "But this isn't a contest."

Morgan smiled at him.

"Hungry?" Kelsey asked her. "There's food in the RV."

"I'll wait for dinner," Morgan said.

"I won't," Tyler said. "Do you want anything, Bob?"

"Nope," Bob said, as Kelsey stood.

"I want to know what else Ryan has hiding in the fridge," she said, joining Tyler. They entered the RV together, and walked into the immaculate kitchen.

"So what do you think I can eat?" Tyler said, opening the fridge, which had a row of neat plastic containers.

"No idea," Kelsey said.

"I wish there were more dumplings, but I know Bob ate every one of them," Tyler said.

"There are still muffins," Kelsey said, spotting them on the counter.

"That will work. All this fresh air is making me hungry," Tyler said. Kelsey handed Tyler a muffin and a paper napkin and took one for herself. She broke off a piece and ate it.

"Did you enjoy the walk?" Kelsey asked Tyler.

"I loved every minute of it," Tyler replied. He kissed her.

"I did too," Kelsey said.

"Why are you so wonderful?" Tyler asked her, taking a bite of his muffin.

Kelsey beamed at him.

"I'm not," she replied.

"You have no idea," Tyler said. "Is this a good vacation for you?"

"It is. I like being with you," Kelsey said.

"I'm glad," Tyler said. He took another bite of his muffin. He chewed thoughtfully, then sighed. "It's our last break for a while, so I'll have to make the most of it."

"Are you?" Kelsey asked.

"I'm pretending Darrow Law School and Bill Simon don't exist. That's making things better," Tyler commented.

"We still have more than a week of vacation."

"Another week of paradise with you," Tyler replied.

They finished their muffins and returned outside.

"We need ice," Bob said as they sat at the table.

"They sell it at the snack bar," Kelsey said. "I can get some."

"I want some limes too. Do you kids want anything?" he asked, standing up.

Tyler shook his head.

"No thanks," Kelsey said.

"Morgan," Bob said.

"Yes?"

Bob took his car keys out his pocket and tossed them to her. Morgan caught them.

"Show me where the grocery store is," he said.

"I can drive? That?" Morgan said, glancing at Bob's Maserati, which was currently parked in front of the RV.

"Sure. Let's go," Bob said. Morgan stood and she and Bob walked to his car and got in. Morgan raced off, Bob in the seat beside her.

Tyler glanced at Kelsey and smiled. "Bob knows where the store is. He's been here a hundred times," he commented.

Kelsey looked into Tyler's amused eyes.

"Morgan?" Kelsey asked, puzzled.

"Bob likes younger women."

Kelsey covered her mouth with her hand in surprise.

"No," she said in shock.

Tyler shrugged. "Don't say later that I didn't tell you."

Ryan and Jessica arrived back at the campsite about 45 minutes later.

"Where's Bob?" he asked, hauling bags out of the car.

"He went to the store with Morgan," Tyler said nonchalantly.

"Morgan's here? Great," Ryan replied.

"What's all of this?" Kelsey asked Ryan. She had spotted three bags from the North Wilderness store.

"We stopped by your parents' store and picked up a few things."

"A few," Kelsey said deadpan.

"Your dad gave me a nice discount," Ryan said, taking out two more bags. Jessica walked around the car, with more bags in her hands.

"The merchants of Port Townsend had a good day today," Tyler commented, taking the bags from Jessica's hands and putting them on the picnic table.

"So much cute stuff," Jessica said. "Who knew you could look fashionable out in the wild?"

"Tyler, if you'll help Jessica, I'll start dinner," Ryan said.

"You didn't get take-out?" Tyler asked.

"I figured I won't cook in Portland, so I might as well cook here. I'm making tacos. It shouldn't take long," Ryan replied. He walked into the RV and Kelsey and Tyler helped Jessica with her bags. Then Tyler took his iPad and walked the few yards over to the outside tables at the campground store to read, while Jessica and Kelsey sat at the campsite picnic table and began to chat about their respective days. Their phones buzzed a few moments later, at the same time.

Zach, who was obviously bored on his vacation, had sent an article via message to the group.

Hell hath no fury as Lisa Olsen scorned

Seattle-

Now that the secret of the thousands of patents owned by Chen Industries is out, if your company is lining up to negotiate a license for one of the patents, you might want to check what your CEO said about the potential deal a few months ago.

Sources say that negotiators for Tactec have been told to add a 25% premium when starting any negotiations with companies whose CEOs are on a list for having called Lisa Olsen out in the media for the Chen deal.

Tactec denies that any such list exists, but corporate sources say that CEOs on the list include Roger Dennison of Mitard Software, who called Ms. Olsen a 'bubblehead' and called the Chen Industries deal a 'rookie move'. Also allegedly on the list is Karen Kane, CEO of Frethe, who called the purchase 'a lesson in stupidity.'

Although at the time of purchase, eyebrows were raised at the inflated price that Tactec paid for Chen Industries, now that the existence of the patents is known, most experts now believe that Tactec will be more than amply rewarded for its daring.

Estimates vary, but the licensing fees that Tactec can expect over the next year alone are likely to be in the millions, and several commentators believe that Tactec will be able to recoup its costs within the next three years, just on licensing fees alone.

Chen Industries founder, Chen Chih-Ming, in an interview after the purchase stated that he was pleased to sell the company to Tactec, because of their commitment to maintaining the family atmosphere of the privately-owned company. He noted that Tactec would be able to monetize the patent portfolio better than he and his small company would have been able to. Mr. Chen also stated in the interview that he looked forward to beginning his new full-time job of golf and travel.

"Why didn't anyone know about the patents?" Jessica asked Kelsey, looking up from her phone.

"U.S. patents are issued in the name of the inventor, not the company," Kelsey replied. "Chen Industries didn't tell anyone about them, so no one knew."

"Then how did Lisa find out?"

Kelsey shook her head. "No idea."

Jessica wrinkled her nose. "And I bet Tyler won't tell me," she commented.

"Probably not," Kelsey said.

"He'd tell you."

"I'm not sure of that. He's not very happy with Collins Nicol right now, and I am working for them next summer."

"You could get it out of him," Jessica said.

"Ask Bob," Kelsey said.

"Bob?"

"He knows, and you're working for him."

"I don't know Bob that well yet," Jessica said.

"Then ask Ryan to ask him."

"Ryan wouldn't ask Bob that. Bob would know it was me. Ask Tyler."

Kelsey laughed. "I'll try to remember. But I'm telling him you asked me."

Bob and Morgan returned to the campsite about a half hour later, just as Ryan had begun bringing out the side dishes for dinner. Morgan stepped out of the driver's seat, radiant.

"That's a nice ride," she said.

"Bob let you drive?" Ryan commented. "I'm not allowed to drive the Maserati."

"Morgan's a better driver than you," Bob said, walking around the car. Morgan gave him back the keys.

"Faster, too," Ryan pouted, going back into the RV.

"Did you get your limes?" Tyler asked, walking back into the campsite. His iPad was in his hand.

"I did, thank you," Bob said.

"A must-have on any camping adventure," Tyler said with sarcasm.

"I know what I like," Bob replied with a smile.

The next morning, Bob invited Tyler and Kelsey to go on a run with him. Ryan and Jessica stayed in the RV, watching old movies.

"So you're Tyler's girl," Bob said to Kelsey as they ran through the woods.

"I suppose," Kelsey replied.

"No, it's a compliment. Tyler's checklist for a suitable girlfriend runs into the hundreds."

"Thousands," Tyler corrected him.

"I never thought you'd find anyone," Bob commented. "You're so picky."

"I have high standards."

"Yeah, that's pretty clear," Bob replied. "Why'd you pick Kelsey?"

"She meets my criteria. And she's hot," Tyler said.

Bob laughed. "So why are you going out with him?" he asked Kelsey.

"I have no idea," Kelsey teased.

"You aren't as picky as I am," Tyler noted. Kelsey giggled.

"No, I guess I'm not," she agreed. "I don't know. Tyler's pretty smart. That's very attractive to me."

"And I'm hot," Tyler added saucily.

"Well, there is that," Kelsey agreed.

"How did you get away from work for a run?" Tyler asked Bob.

"Carol scheduled a phantom meeting for me. I'm busy until one," Bob said.

"Nice. I want a Carol," Tyler said.

"Ask your mother. I'm sure she'll arrange one for you," Bob replied.

"It wouldn't work. 'I'm sorry, Mr. Olsen can't attend your boring class today. He has a meeting.'"

Bob laughed. "Well, you're almost done with second-year. I'd say it was all downhill from here, but you're Law Review editor next year, so you're out of luck."

"I know. I wanted it, but now I'm reconsidering the wisdom of being editor."

"Well, you have a girlfriend now," Bob said.

"I do," Tyler said, looking at Kelsey.

"What do you want to do after graduation?" Bob asked Kelsey.

"I'm not sure yet. Maybe patents, or licensing. Definitely something in intellectual property."

"Kelsey wants to be the next Lisa Olsen," Tyler interjected.

"IP is where your mother got started," Bob said. "So that's not a bad plan."

"Did you work in IP too?" Kelsey asked him.

"No. White-collar crime defense," Bob replied.

"How did you meet Tyler's mom then? Did you work at the same firm?" Kelsey asked.

"We met through our spouses," Bob replied. "Ryan's mom was an aerobics instructor and Chris was a client in her gym. They got to talking, discovered that Lisa and I were both lawyers in town and suggested we meet each other."

"Really?" Kelsey said, glancing at Tyler, who nodded.

"The rest is history," Tyler said.

Kelsey and Tyler spent almost two hours running with Bob, then they returned to the campsite, where Ryan had once again prepared lunch.

"I think you need to move back home, so you can cook for me," Bob commented to Ryan, who beamed.

Bob went back to work after lunch, and the rest went to the playground and flew Tyler's kite. After a half hour, Ryan returned to the RV, complaining about the cold. Jessica stayed with Tyler and Kelsey, and the three of them headed to the beach.

"Tyler, did you read Zach's article?" Jessica said, nudging Kelsey, who sighed.

"I did."

"Is it true?" Jessica asked him.

"The list? Probably," Tyler replied. Jessica nudged Kelsey again.

"Tyler, Jessica wants to know how your mom knew about the patents," Kelsey said. Jessica glared at her, and Kelsey grinned.

"Sorry, that's a secret, Jess," Tyler said.

"You have a lot of secrets, Mr. Olsen," Jessica said.

"Do I? Sorry. My mother trusts me with a lot of private corporate information."

"You'd tell Kelsey."

"I don't tell her everything. Also, Kelsey works for Collins Nicol. They have a legal responsibility to keep Tactec information private."

"I'm going to work for Tactec this summer," Jessica said.

"Then you'll be privy to a lot of information I don't have access to. Bob runs his office separately from my mom's," Tyler pointed out.

"No fair," Jessica pouted.

"I apologize, Miss Hunter," Tyler said.

"See if I tell you anything about Bob," she said.

"Considering what you're likely to find out, I'm not sure I want to know," Tyler commented.

Morgan arrived to the campsite a few hours later. Ryan had made a special dinner of roast pork to honor their last night of camping.

"This has been a memorable vacation," Bob said, looking at Jessica.

"I hate to admit it, but I'm actually feeling relaxed," Jessica said sheepishly.

"No," Kelsey teased.

"It's true."

"Told you," Kelsey said.

"Not as relaxed as Tyler, though. It looks like you can barely stand," Jessica noted.

"I didn't realize life could be like this," Tyler said. "I've read three books, eaten great food, and slept under the stars. I don't want to leave."

"You aren't going to turn into one of those people on the Discovery Channel, renouncing civilization and moving to the woods, are you?" Jessica asked in concern.

"No," Tyler said. "Someone from Tactec would find me anyway."

"That's true," Bob commented. "Have you had a good time, Ryan?"

"It's been nice. I've enjoyed being in the kitchen," Ryan replied.

"As have we all," Kelsey commented.

"Yes, thank you, Ryan. I was afraid we'd be eating freeze-dried granola for dinner," Jessica said.

"I want you to teach Margaret how to make *varenyky*," Bob said.

"I can't imagine teaching Margaret anything," Ryan said in awe.

"Margaret thinks that the only heritage food is lutefisk. I'm not eating jellied cod," Bob commented.

"It's traditional," Tyler said.

"Will you eat it?" Bob asked him.

"No," Tyler said, laughing.

"I'm glad you guys came out to visit us," Morgan said. "It will be boring without you."

"No it won't," Kelsey said. "Anyway, I'll see you soon."

"Seattle in May," Morgan replied.

"Please talk Jazz out of the bright pink bridesmaid dresses," Kelsey said.

"I've tried everything, babe, but she's determined."

"Have you talked to Mama?" Kelsey said. "Gone over Jasmine's head?"

"Mama Jefferson just laughed. She's going to let her precious little girl ruin our lives," Morgan said, slicing into her meat.

"I can't wait for this wedding," Tyler said.

"If you take pictures of me in a pink bridesmaid dress, I'll never forgive you," Kelsey warned him.

"What's so wrong with pink?" Jessica asked.

"If you were a bridesmaid, nothing. Bright pink looks great on you. But Morgan and I are going to look washed-out and awful," Kelsey replied.

"Why is Jasmine doing this, then?" Jessica asked.

"Because behind that angelic face, she's pure evil. At least when it comes to this wedding. Bridezilla in our midst," Morgan commented.

"I just can't wait until May," Kelsey said with sarcasm.

After dinner, Ryan and Jessica walked to the beach facing Port Townsend, Bob and Morgan sat at the picnic table talking, and Tyler took Kelsey and the wool blanket to the other side of the campground, to the beach facing Indian Island. She cuddled in his arms, and he wrapped the blanket around the two of them.

"I love you," Tyler said, as they sat quietly, watching the waves.

"I love you too, Tyler," Kelsey said.

"I'll always treasure this time with you. Thank you for sharing your town with me," Tyler said.

"Any time," Kelsey replied.

The next morning, Kelsey and Tyler packed up the tents. They rolled up the sleeping bags and placed them back into the giant plastic box her father had provided.

"Some of this stuff is wet," Tyler said to her.

"It's condensation. It's okay, my dad will hang it in our backyard to dry before he stores it," Kelsey said.

They finished taking everything out of the tents, and packed everything away.

"How do you disassemble the tents? Can I watch?" Tyler asked.

"Of course," Kelsey grinned. She walked to one of the tents, unsnapped a buckle, and pulled out one pole. The tent collapsed in front of their eyes.

"That's it? That's all that was between me and the tent falling down on me at night?" Jessica asked. She had been sitting at the picnic table drinking coffee. Ryan was inside the RV, talking to Bob.

"That's it," Kelsey said, sliding the pole out from the folds of the tent fabric. "Here, you can help. Fold this up," Kelsey said to Tyler, handing him the pole.

"Really?" Tyler said, excitedly. Kelsey glanced at his sparkling eyes. He was like a little kid out here.

Bob and Ryan left the RV and sat at the table with Jessica.

"It was nice having you kids here," Bob said to them.

"You go back tonight?" Kelsey asked, as she heaped the wet tent into her arms and stuffed it into a garbage bag. Her father would take it out of the garbage bag at home and let it dry in the backyard.

"I do," Bob said.

"We should vacation together again soon," Ryan said.

"You like vacationing with your old man?"

"You aren't old," Ryan said.

"Thanks," Bob said.

"Thank you for loaning us your condo in Portland," Jessica said.

"You're welcome. Someone might as well get some use out of it," Bob commented.

"When was the last time you were there?" Kelsey asked him.

"I've slept in that condo once," Bob said.

"That's surprising," Tyler said. He had finished folding the poles and had packed them back in their storage bag.

"I don't get to Portland much," Bob said. "And when I do, I usually just fly back up to Seattle and sleep in my own bed. Anyway, I'm always in Arizona lately."

"Isn't that acquisition almost done?" Ryan asked him.

"Almost," Bob said. "When is your father coming to pick up the tents, Kelsey? I'd like to be around to say goodbye to him."

"He said around 5:30. The store closes at 5 and he's the only one there today."

"Great. I'll still be here then," Bob said.

"What will you do without us?" Jessica asked.

"Watch the birds. Walk on the beach. Work," Bob replied. Jessica giggled.

They all finished packing everything for Mr. North and placed their own things in the boys' cars. Kelsey took the last of the chocolate chip muffins, and put her Kindle front and center in her bag for Portland. It was almost a four-hour drive, and one she had made many times before. She had always wanted to fly, but since it was almost two hours from here to Seatac Airport, it really didn't make sense.

Everyone said goodbye to Bob, who gave everyone hugs and looked a little sad to see them all leave. Then Ryan and Jess got into Ryan's car, and Tyler and Kelsey got into his Audi and they drove out of the campsite.

Ryan led the way slowly.

"Ryan got a ticket yesterday," Tyler confided to Kelsey. "So he's taking no chances."

"I was wondering," Kelsey said, smiling.

Tyler drove them out of the state park, through Indian Island and Port Hadlock. They passed the QFC grocery store. But to Kelsey's surprise, when they reached route 19, they didn't turn left, south to Portland. Instead, they turned right, heading to Port Townsend.

"Where are we going?" Kelsey asked Tyler.

"It's a surprise," Tyler said.

"Are we going to Port Townsend?" Kelsey asked him.

"It's a surprise," Tyler repeated. "Ryan's not dealing with these questions," he commented.

"Jessica doesn't know this area," Kelsey said. She looked out of the window, as they passed stores and places she had passed hundreds of times before as a young girl.

As she had predicted, they drove back into Port Townsend, but to her surprise, Tyler followed Ryan into the Jefferson County International Airport. Although it was an international airport — thanks to its proximity to Canada — it was tiny and little more than a landing strip, although a very serviceable one.

Kelsey looked at Tyler, puzzled.

"Are we going to the Aero Museum?" she asked. There was a very nice historical museum on the airport grounds. Tyler had already driven past the airport restaurant.

"Patience, Miss North," Tyler said. He followed Ryan and parked the Audi next to one of the hangars. "We're here," he said, brightly. "Bring your bag."

Before Kelsey could ask any more questions, Tyler had hopped out of the Audi, his own duffel bag in his hands. Kelsey followed him out, holding her own bag. She walked over to Jessica, who looked as puzzled as she felt. In the meantime, Ryan was shaking hands with someone in a airplane captain uniform. Then he introduced Tyler to the captain, who shook hands with him as well.

"What's going on?" Jessica asked Kelsey.

"No idea," Kelsey replied.

"Come over," Ryan called to them. The girls followed, travel bags in hand.

"This is Captain McAdams," Ryan said, introducing them. "Captain, this is Jessica and Kelsey."

"Lovely to meet you," he said, shaking both of their hands.

"The captain will be flying us to Portland," Tyler said to them. Both girls looked at Tyler in shock.

"Surprise," Tyler grinned.

"We're flying?" Jessica asked, as the captain turned and headed toward a plane sitting on the tarmac.

"Yes!" Ryan said, throwing an arm around Jessica and leading her to the plane.

"Kelsey's always wanted to fly to Portland," Tyler said, gently taking Kelsey's hand, and following Ryan.

Kelsey opened her mouth, then closed it. It was true, but she hadn't expected that they would be flying today. This was a real surprise.

They followed the captain to the small plane, where an assistant took their bags and placed them in the back of the plane.

"Who wants the front?" Ryan said brightly.

Jessica looked at him in shock. "Are you kidding me?" Ryan shrugged.

"Are we really flying?" Kelsey asked.

"We are," Tyler said. "Get in."

Still stunned, the girls got into the plane. There were five soft ivory-colored leather seats, one for the pilot, and four passenger seats in an L-shape. Their bags had been stored in the back, behind the back two seats. Jessica sat in one of the back seats, Kelsey in the other. Tyler took the seat in the front, next to the pilot, and Ryan sat in the lone seat between Tyler in the front and the girls in the back.

Captain McAdams spoke to the ground crew, and got into the plane. Everyone was fitted with headsets, and the captain spoke.

"Welcome aboard. Today we'll be flying from Jefferson County International Airport to Pearson Field in Vancouver, Washington. Our expected travel time is 29 minutes. Please make sure your seat belts are fastened," he said.

"Are you okay, Jess?" Ryan asked her playfully, glancing back from his own seat.

Jessica made the sign of the cross.

Once they were airborne, Kelsey finally opened her eyes and looked out of the window next to her. She was holding hands with Jessica, but it wasn't clear which of them was holding the other's hand more tightly. As they passed over the fields and farms of Western Washington, she marveled at the view.

Here she was, Kelsey North, second-year law student, being ferried to Portland, Oregon by private jet, because of an offhand comment that she had made about flying there. She glanced at the front. Tyler was looking with interest out of the front window, while Ryan was fighting sleep, and losing, in the seat behind Tyler.

She had to admit, despite her fear — which still hadn't left her — that it was a beautiful flight. Captain McAdams was clearly a very skilled pilot, and the sky was clear and bright. Kelsey glanced at Jessica, who had also opened her eyes and was finally looking around.

Faster than she expected, they had been cleared for landing at Pearson Field and Captain McAdams expertly glided them down.

"Thank you," Kelsey heard Jessica whisper as the wheels touched down.

A few minutes later, the group of four stood by a limousine as their bags were placed in the trunk. Ryan and Tyler were shaking Captain McAdams' hand.

"We'll see you next week," Ryan said happily. He had slept on the flight, and was bright-eyed again.

"Next week?" Jessica asked.

"We have to go back to Seattle," Tyler reminded her.

"Right," Jessica said timidly.

Kelsey hugged Jessica's shoulders, ignoring her own stomach butterflies. "It will be fun," she said.

"Right," Jessica repeated.

"Come on, let's go," Tyler said. They got into the limousine and the driver drove off.

"How was it?" Tyler asked Kelsey.

She paused before answering. She had been terrified, at least for a while, but it had been an incredible experience.

"It was awesome," she concluded. "Thank you."

Tyler kissed her hair.

"Was that Bob's plane?" Kelsey asked.

"The old one," Ryan said. Jessica was leaning her head on his shoulder. "He's having a new one delivered this summer."

"Did the pilot say we were landing in Washington State? I thought we were going to Portland," Jessica said.

"We're in Vancouver, Washington," Kelsey explained. "It's right across the Columbia River from Portland. Look out the window, we'll cross it soon."

As if on cue, a few minutes later the limousine crossed over the

Columbia River and drove into Portland. Jessica looked out of the window.

"Is that a streetcar?" she asked Kelsey excitedly.

"Yes, Portland has an extensive streetcar system," Kelsey replied. "One of them goes through Portland State's campus."

"So cute," Jessica said, smiling.

"You'll like Portland," Kelsey said.

"That's what you said about camping," Jessica commented.

"Portland's a city. You'll love it," Kelsey said.

"We'll see," Jessica replied.

Less than fifteen minutes later, the limousine pulled up in front of a large building, in what was clearly a hip neighborhood.

"We'll drop our bags and come right back out," Ryan said to Jessica, who was looking around. "I know Tyler wants to go to the bookstore."

"You bet I do. It's one of the best ones in the country," Tyler replied. Their driver pulled out their bags, which the boys took, and they all thanked him and walked into the building.

"Good afternoon, Mr. Perkins," the concierge said pleasantly.

"Hi," Ryan said. They walked through the granite lobby and took the elevator to the seventh floor. They got off the elevator and walked to the condo.

"It's a little small," Ryan warned the girls. He opened the door to a spacious condo.

"It's still bigger than my house," Jessica commented. She put her bag down on the floor, and the girls looked around. It was a two-bedroom, two-bath condo, with an additional office and a large walk-in closet. The kitchen was large and well-equipped, and unlike Ryan's condo in Seattle, there was a huge south-facing patio. Kelsey and Tyler walked out onto it and looked at the view.

"Spectacular," Tyler said.

"I'm so excited to be back in Portland," Kelsey said.

"You'll have to give me the tour," Tyler said, wrapping his arms around her waist and nuzzling her.

"I can't wait," Kelsey said, nuzzling him back.

Within a few minutes, the group had sorted out their sleeping arrangements. Kelsey and Jess would share the master bedroom, Ryan would take the smaller bedroom, while Tyler would sleep on the pull-out sofa in the living room.

"It's tiny," Ryan groused.

"Didn't he buy it before he married Charlotte?" Tyler asked. "How many bedrooms does he need?"

"He knew I'd borrow it," Ryan replied.

"Another reason not to have space for a lot of people," Tyler pointed out.

Ryan laughed. "I guess you have a point," he said, slipping his Darrow Law sweatshirt over his head. "Are you two ready?" he asked.

"Ready," Jessica said.

"Remember our deal, Miss North," Tyler said quietly to her as they followed Ryan and Jess out of the condo.

"What deal?" Kelsey asked, as Ryan pressed the button for the elevator.

"You paid for the camping trip and I pay for Portland."

Kelsey frowned.

"I bought you a kite and a cup of coffee," she said.

"A deal's a deal," Tyler said brightly. They followed Ryan and Jess onto the elevator.

"We're in the Pearl District," Ryan was telling Jessica. "It's one of the coolest neighborhoods in Portland."

"It is," Kelsey said.

"Tyler likes it because there's a gigantic bookstore and a Whole Foods. He doesn't need to leave the Pearl," Ryan teased.

"Ha, ha," Tyler said. "I guess it's pretty much true though."

"When were you last in Portland?" Kelsey asked.

"College?" Tyler asked Ryan.

"Before Charlotte," Ryan replied.

"B.C.?" Jessica joked.

Ryan shook his head. "My mother's name starts with a C too."

"Right," Jess said. "It's hard to keep track."

"For Bob too," Tyler quipped. The elevator opened and they walked out into the lobby.

"Excuse me, Mr. Perkins?" the concierge said politely.

"Yes?" Ryan said, walking over to the desk. Everyone followed him. The concierge was looking for something, then looked up at him.

"Your car has been serviced," she said, handing him a set of keys. "It's parked in your slot in the basement. A-2."

"Great," Ryan said, taking the keys and pocketing them.

"I'm sorry, but do you mind if I ask you a question?" she asked.

"Okay."

"Do you go to Darrow Law School?"

"We all do. These are my friends, Tyler, Kelsey and my girlfriend, Jessica," he said.

The concierge looked at them in awe.

"All of you go to Darrow? That's the best law school in the country," She said. "What year are you?"

"Second." Ryan replied.

"You made it through first year. Congratulations. My sister wanted to go to Darrow, but she couldn't get in. She's at Columbia."

"Better her than me," Jessica whispered to Kelsey.

"Anyway," the concierge said, "Very impressive. I hope you all enjoy your stay in Portland."

"Thank you," Ryan said. He led the group out of the lobby and onto the street.

"What's really impressive that the four of us are 5% of the second-year class," Tyler commented.

"At least no one else has failed out this year," Kelsey said.

"Darrow does most of their cutting during first year," Tyler said. "At this point, everyone will probably graduate."

"Except Zachary," Ryan called over his shoulder, as they crossed the street.

Tyler laughed. "You think you're so smart," he said.

"I am, compared to Zach," Ryan retorted.

"Don't be a hater. He's trying."

"Of course he isn't," Ryan said.

"No, he isn't. He's not as inspired as you," Tyler commented.

Ryan looked at Jessica lovingly. "I suppose," he conceded.

Jessica smiled at Ryan. "I thought your car was in Port Townsend," she said, referring to the keys he had just been handed. "Or did someone fly that down too?"

"Our cars are being driven back to school. Bob keeps a car at every condo," Ryan said. "She gave me the keys to the one he keeps here."

"Of course. So a car's been sitting in the lot, as unused as the condo?" Jessica asked.

"He doesn't like to rent," Ryan shrugged.

"I'm starting to think there's a thing as too much money," Jessica mused.

"Bite your tongue, Miss Hunter," Ryan grinned.

"Where are we going?" Tyler asked. Kelsey didn't care where they were headed, personally. It was so nice to be back in Portland.

"I was wondering that too," Jessica said. "There's so many cute places around here."

"We can look around later," Ryan said. "I want to go to Whole Foods so I can decide what to cook."

"I thought you weren't cooking here?" Tyler asked, as they crossed another street.

"We have to eat breakfast," Ryan said. "Come along."

"The cooking store that you like in Pike Place Market has a branch here," Kelsey said as they walked by it.

Ryan looked up. "We'll go later," he said.

They crossed the street and were standing outside of Whole Foods. Tyler looked back at the condo.

"I had no idea Bob's condo was so close," he commented.

"Where did you stay when you were down here if you didn't stay at Bob's?" Kelsey asked.

"The Hilton," Tyler said.

"That seems a little tame for Ryan," Kelsey said.

"Portland is a little tame for Ryan," Tyler said. They followed Ryan and Jessica into the store. Ryan looked around at the produce, while Tyler looked at his phone, then placed it back in his pocket.

"Nothing's really in season yet," Ryan said in disappointment. Jessica was looking at an Easter lily in a bright yellow pot. "How am I going to make scones?"

"We're in a crisis," Tyler commented. Ryan glared at him.

"You could use frozen berries," Jessica said.

"Ick," Ryan said.

"Hazelnuts are always in season in Oregon," Kelsey noted.

"Now that's an idea I can use," Ryan said brightly. "Come on, Jess."

"Add chocolate," Tyler said.

"You'll be lucky to get a scone," Ryan snapped. He walked off, holding Jessica's hand. Tyler chuckled.

"Do you want anything?" Tyler asked Kelsey. "I'm getting hungry."

"It is lunchtime," Kelsey noted. "I can't believe we were at the campground less than two hours ago." She smiled at him. "That was really cool. Thank you."

"I'm glad you enjoyed it. Why should Bob be the only one who plays with his toys?" Tyler said.

"It's nice that he's willing to share," Kelsey said.

"Bob's getting older. I think he's thinking about what's next for him," Tyler said.

"Do you think he'll retire?" Kelsey asked, as they walked through the aisles, hand in hand.

"Never. But he might slow down a little," Tyler commented. They spotted Ryan and Jessica looking at the nut and dried-fruit bins.

"Are we going to eat soon, Ryan, or should I get something?" Tyler asked him as they walked up.

"Hold your horses. I'll only be a few minutes," Ryan said impatiently.

"The master at his craft," Tyler commented. Ryan stuck his tongue out at Tyler. "Very adult," Tyler said.

"Kelsey," Ryan said, deliberately ignoring Tyler. "What do you think? Roasted or buy raw and toast them myself?"

"Buy roasted. We're not going to notice the difference," Kelsey said.

"We're philistines," Tyler said.

"I'm warning you, Tyler Olsen," Ryan said.

"Sorry. I'm just hungry. *Mea culpa,*" Tyler said.

"Okay. We'll come back," Ryan said. "If Tyler's speaking Latin, he must be starving."

"Where are we eating?" Jessica asked.

"There's a brewpub down the street," Ryan said. He took her hand again and led them out of the store.

"The grocery store's open until 10," Jessica noted.

"Perfect," Ryan said. They walked down the street and entered a big brewpub.

"You have a very good sense of direction," Kelsey said to Ryan once they were seated. Ryan seemed to know Portland as well as New York.

"True," Tyler said, looking at his menu.

"I don't want Jess to get lost," Ryan said. Jessica smiled at him.

"I want everything," Tyler said. "I'm starving."

"We ate like pigs when we were camping," Jessica noted. "I never thought we'd make a dent in all the food you bought."

"It's the fresh air," Kelsey said.

"Kels. They have poutine," Ryan said. pointing to the menu.

"What's poutine?" Jessica asked Ryan.

"Cheese fries with gravy," he said. "Kelsey and I had it last summer, but I haven't gotten around to making it for you."

"You guys did everything fun last summer," Jessica pouted.

"This summer you can do it with us," Kelsey said brightly.

"Let's order poutine," Tyler said. "I want chili fries too."

"You are hungry," Jessica said in amusement.

"And onion rings," Kelsey added. "We'll have to go running this week," she said to Tyler.

"I bet you know some great places to run around here," Tyler commented as Ryan signaled for the waitress.

"McCall Waterfront Park is beautiful, and if we're lucky, the cherry blossoms will be out," Kelsey said.

The waitress arrived and they placed their order. Tyler leaned on his arm and looked at Kelsey. "So what do you want to do while we're here?" he asked.

"Be with you," Kelsey said. Tyler grinned.

"So cute," Ryan teased.

"Shut up. You're just jealous," Tyler replied.

"I can't say that about you any more now that you're finally dating Kelsey," Ryan commented.

"No, you can't," Tyler said.

"It took you long enough," Jessica said.

"I had some things to work out, Miss Hunter. Miss North understood," Tyler said.

"I suppose," Jessica said. "So Kelsey, where are you taking me?"

"Where do you want to go?" Kelsey asked.

"Well, since the dress code here seems to be about the same as Seattle, I'm wondering if there's any point of going clothes shopping."

"Actually, there are some beautiful boutiques in the Pearl," Kelsey said.

Jessica wrinkled her nose. "I probably should resist. I'm supposed to be saving for tuition."

"I'll pay for whatever you want here," Ryan said fingering her auburn curls.

"No, you won't. We're not going through a replay of Spring Break in New York," Jessica said.

"I'm paying for Kelsey," Tyler said brightly.

"That's what you think," Kelsey replied.

"We had a deal," Tyler replied petulantly as their drinks were placed on the table.

"Ha," Kelsey said, taking a sip of her Coke.

"Are you two really going to make us go through this again?" Ryan asked. "Let us pay here, and we'll go back to normal at Darrow."

"Where you two insist on paying for everything there," Jessica said to him.

"Well, yeah," Ryan said.

"No," Kelsey said.

"Why not?" Ryan asked.

"You guys cheat. Taking us to the most expensive restaurant in New York City. Like we weren't supposed to notice," Jessica replied.

Ryan looked at Tyler.

"You weren't supposed to notice," Tyler commented.

"Did you really pay two thousand dollars for dinner?" Jessica asked him.

"I'm taking the fifth," Tyler said.

"I knew it," Jessica replied.

"This is Portland, Jess. There's nothing like that here," Ryan said.

"Forget it," she replied.

Their appetizers arrived. The poutine was gooey with melted cheese curds, and the onion rings were golden brown and crispy. Tyler stuck his fork into the chili fries as the server walked away.

"Jessica, do you know how much money I get a month for an allowance?" Tyler asked before he placed a waffle fry into his mouth.

"No," Jessica replied.

Tyler looked at Kelsey as he chewed. "You are good at keeping information confidential, Miss North," he said to her.

Kelsey knew the number because Tyler had been asked at his deposition. She still couldn't believe that he got around one hundred thousand dollars a year as an allowance. Kelsey got about one hundred bucks a month.

"Trust me, a fifty-dollar meal isn't going to break me," Tyler said, taking an onion ring.

"I get three times what Tyler does," Ryan said, taking an onion ring of his own.

"At least," Tyler replied.

Kelsey looked at Ryan in shock.

"Are you kidding me?" Kelsey blurted out. Bob gave Ryan over a quarter of a million dollars a year? No wonder he managed to get into so much trouble.

"Let us pay," Tyler said, biting into his onion ring.

Jessica, who had no idea of the huge numbers that they were batting around, took a forkful of poutine.

"No," she said.

Ryan sighed.

"When you marry me, you'll accept my presents," he commented.

"I'm not marrying you," Jessica replied.

"Of course you are, you just don't know it yet," Ryan said confidently.

Jessica smiled at him.

Tyler wiped his fingers on his napkin and pulled out his smartphone. He typed some numbers into the calculator on it.

"Jessica, in the five minutes we've been arguing about this, my mother has earned my entire allowance for the month. If I paid for everything, and I do mean everything, that you and Kelsey want over the week, I'd probably spend a tenth of my allowance. Thirty seconds of my mother's time. Stop arguing and let us pay for you," Tyler said, placing his smartphone on the table.

"Really, Jess. This is silly. You too, Kelsey," Ryan said.

"I'll think about it," Jessica said, taking an onion ring. Tyler's phone buzzed. He glanced at it, then took another chili fry.

"Where else do you want to go, Jess?" Kelsey asked her, returning to the previous subject.

"I'd like to find a knitting store. I really enjoyed knitting Ryan's present. It was very relaxing."

"Really?" Kelsey asked doubtfully. She didn't find knitting relaxing at all.

"Really," Jessica said. "My nephews are getting a little old for hand-knit hats though, so I need to think of something else."

"I liked mine," Ryan said.

"Me, too," Tyler said, smiling at Kelsey.

"There's a window where handmade gifts aren't appreciated," Jessica explained. "My nephews are getting to that age. I can knit for them again when they hit their twenties. I was thinking that maybe I'd knit newborn hats for the hospital."

"Newborn hats?" Ryan asked.

"Babies lose a lot of heat from their heads, so they put hats on them, particularly in the newborn intensive care unit. The hats are so tiny, I could probably make one in an hour or two, which would be a perfect stress reliever, " Jessica said.

"That's really nice," Tyler said. Ryan hugged Jessica's shoulders.

"I'll make sure we find a knitting store for you," Kelsey said. "How about you two? What do you want to do?"

"Bookstore and a tour of your college for me," Tyler said.

"I don't have anything," Ryan said. "Except maybe the cooking store."

"We should go to the Saturday market too," Kelsey said. "They always have great stuff."

"I think I'm going to Mass on Easter," Jessica said. "Is there a church near here?"

"I'll look," Tyler said, picking up his phone.

"Do you want me to come?" Ryan asked her.

Jessica shook her head. "It's okay. I know you aren't religious," she replied.

"There's one a few blocks away, Jess. St. Andre's," Tyler said, setting down the phone.

"Thanks, Tyler. I'll call over later and see what time Mass is," Jessica said.

They finished the appetizers, then their lunch arrived. Tyler gave Kelsey a bite of his reuben, then dove into it himself, while the girls ate their pizzas. Ryan poked around his chopped salad.

"Jess?" he asked.

"Yes?" Jessica asked. She was taking a piece of sausage off the pizza.

"Why do you want to go to Mass?" Ryan asked her.

"I don't know. I just feel like I should. I didn't go last year at Easter."

"I see," Ryan said. Jessica ate the sausage.

"Maybe she needs spiritual strength to deal with you." Tyler quipped.

"Going out with me is a religious experience," Ryan replied.

"Don't be blasphemous," Jessica said.

"Sorry," Ryan said.

"I don't know, Ryan," Jessica continued. "Maybe I'm feeling a little guilty."

"About what?" Kelsey asked.

"About defying my father," Jessica replied. "I'm supposed to be in New York right now, not with you."

Ryan looked at her and stroked her face. "Do you want to go back?" he asked her.

Jessica shook her head. "No," she replied. "I want to stay at Darrow. And I want to be with you. It's just hard. I'm not used to doing what I want to do."

"You're an adult," Tyler said.

"I know," Jessica said. "It's a new feeling."

After lunch, they decided to walk around the Pearl District.

"We're buying things for the two of you," Tyler said, as they waited to cross the street. He held Kelsey's hand firmly, as her blonde hair blew in the wind.

"We're not arguing anymore," Ryan agreed.

"You bought lunch," Jessica said. "That's enough."

"Thirty seconds of my mother's time, Jessica," Tyler reminded her.

"Tyler, I appreciate your and Ryan's kindness. I really do. But I can pay my own way," Jessica said.

"Me, too," Kelsey said.

Tyler glared at her. "Fine," he said, stopping on the sidewalk. "Ryan, give me your wallet."

Ryan pulled his wallet out and gave it to Tyler. Tyler took out several bills. Having seen the contents of Ryan's wallet previously, Kelsey was sure Tyler had removed at least seven hundred dollars. Tyler gave the wallet back to Ryan, who returned it to his pocket. Tyler took the money he had taken from Ryan, and placed it in his own pocket.

"Jessica, who is the person you dislike the most at Darrow?"

"Dave Jensen," Jessica said without missing a beat. "I almost had to stay at Darrow last summer to retake Legal Writing after he threatened to fail me over three spelling errors."

"Kelsey?" Tyler asked her.

"You know it's Professor Eliot," she said.

"Okay. I've taken some money out of Ryan's wallet. I'm going to match it. If the two of you don't spend all of it over the next week, I'm going to take the remainder, split it in half, and send one half to Jensen and the other half to Eliot, with your names, and a note saying how much you loved their class."

"Eliot's not going to take money," Kelsey scoffed.

"Dave would," Jessica said under her breath.

"I'll have Jeffrey buy something appropriate. Perhaps an engraved vase. 'Thank you to the best Contracts professor in the world. Love, Kelsey North.'"

Kelsey looked at Tyler. "You wouldn't," she said.

"Try me," Tyler replied sinisterly.

Kelsey looked at Tyler's brown eyes.

"How much money did you take?" Jessica asked.

Tyler shook his head. "I'm not telling."

Kelsey bit her lip. "You're serious, aren't you?" she finally said.

"It's the only way the two of you will stop this nonsense," Tyler said. Ryan grinned.

"You took at least seven hundred dollars out of Ryan's wallet," Kelsey guessed. Tyler smiled.

"At least," he replied.

"You're really mean, Tyler Olsen," she said.

"Better start shopping, Miss North," Tyler said, taking her hand.

"Do you think Tyler is serious?" Jessica asked Kelsey, as they glanced around a shop selling handcrafted jewelry. The boys were standing outside, talking.

Kelsey sighed. "Yeah, I do," she finally concluded.

"How much money do you think he took?"

"At least fifteen hundred total. I'm pretty sure he took seven hundred from Ryan."

"How are we going to spend that kind of money in Portland, Oregon?" Jessica said.

"I have no idea," Kelsey said.

"I will die of embarrassment if Tyler follows through on his threat. Dave Jensen's still on campus, working for Professor Rhodes. I hide every time I see him," Jessica confided.

"I know. I'm always ducking behind shrubbery when I see Eliot. I'm still afraid of her calling on me," Kelsey said.

"Why are they doing this?" Jessica said.

"I guess they're really tired of arguing with us over money," Kelsey said.

"I suppose they have a point. It's not their money. Do you really think Lisa Olsen makes Tyler's entire allowance in five minutes?"

"Yeah, I do. A billion dollars is a lot of money, and she's got several times that," Kelsey said.

Jessica sighed. "I can't believe this," she said. She walked out of the store with Kelsey. Ryan took Jessica's hand. Tyler offered his hand to Kelsey, but she glared at him instead of taking it.

"Is there a problem, Miss North?" Tyler asked brightly.

"You wouldn't really do that to me," she said, crossing her arms.

"We just want to have a good time. You and Miss Hunter are ruining it for us with your incessant arguments over paying for things," Tyler replied.

"But we can buy our own stuff," Jessica said.

"There you go again, Miss Hunter. Fine. I'm sure Mr. Jensen will appreciate the gift," Tyler threatened. "He probably doesn't make that much working for Professor Rhodes. It will be a nice bonus for him."

"I don't like you any more, Tyler," Jessica said.

"Miss North didn't like me at all when we met. That didn't stop me," Tyler replied.

Kelsey surveyed Tyler with her eyes. She had no doubt that he was serious about this. "I give up," she finally said. "What do you want us to do?"

"Have fun. Stop offering to pay for things. Stop putting things back on the shelf because it costs three dollars more than you want to spend," Tyler replied.

"Okay," Kelsey said.

"Jess?" Tyler asked her.

"Okay," Jessica replied.

"Great!" Ryan said. Tyler offered his hand back to Kelsey, who took it this time. Tyler kissed her hand.

"Now we can begin our vacation," Tyler said.

The group continued wandering through the Pearl District. The girls stopped at a store that sold Scandinavian organic cotton clothing.

"Pretty," Ryan said, as Jessica tried on a bright-colored sweater.

"Hmm," Jessica said. Tyler glanced at her.

"It's the wrong color, Tyler. I'm not buying something I hate just to please you," Jessica said.

"Just checking that you're following the rules, Miss Hunter," Tyler said.

"Maybe I'll buy so much I'll bankrupt you," Jessica said.

"That would be difficult," Tyler grinned.

A few blocks later, they walked into a big, beautiful sporting goods store.

"I love all of the wood," Jessica said, looking around.

Tyler stopped to look at a green jacket.

"Planning your next camping trip, Mr. Olsen?" Kelsey asked him.

"With you," he replied. He put the green jacket back on the hook.

"I don't know, I'm still pretty upset about this spending thing," she replied.

"You'll get over it," Tyler said.

"Why does it matter so much to you?"

"I really don't like discussing money so much," Tyler said. "It reminds me of being with Chris. He's obsessed with money too."

"Oh. I guess I hadn't thought of that," Kelsey said. "Sorry."

"Anyway, I don't want you two to deny yourself things. Ryan and I buy whatever we want. You can do that too."

"Our parents aren't billionaires."

"Your boyfriends are," Tyler replied.

"That's not why we're dating you."

"We know that. Trust me, we'd be a lot less generous if we thought you were after our money."

Kelsey giggled. "I don't know about that. Kim got a trip to London."

Tyler laughed. "I guess that's true. Kim's special to Ryan, though. She can get away with anything."

"Interesting," Kelsey said.

"So do you see anything you want?"

"No."

Tyler looked at her severely.

"Tyler, my parents own a sporting goods store. There's nothing I need or want here."

"Okay."

"If I see something I want on this trip, I'll tell you," Kelsey said.

"You promise?"

"I promise," Kelsey said. Tyler held her hand, and they began to walk toward the door.

"Wait, I see something I want," Kelsey said, stopping on the floor.

"What?" Tyler asked her.

Kelsey kissed him.

"You," she replied.

They walked over to an ice cream shop next to Jamison Square Park. Kelsey got peanut-butter-and-jelly ice cream, Tyler got a double scoop of birthday cake and Belgian chocolate, Jessica got a chocolate sundae with cinnamon-toast ice cream and Ryan got spicy-Thai-peanut ice cream.

"These flavors are nuts," Jessica said, as they sat in the park and tried each other's ice cream.

"I love yours," Kelsey said to Ryan.

"Yeah, it's good. I wonder if Kimmy would like the jelly with the peanut butter ice cream. Not that she can eat it," Ryan mused.

"Is all of Portland like this?" Jessica asked.

"Like what?" Kelsey asked.

"Quirky," Jessica asked.

"Yes," Kelsey laughed.

"I love it," Jessica said, eating a spoonful of ice cream.

"Really?" Ryan said.

"Yeah, I'm shocked too," Jessica said. "But there's a surprise around every corner. I love that."

"I'm glad you do," Kelsey said.

"Portland's your city too," Jessica said.

"I had a great time here," Kelsey said.

Although Port Townsend would always be home, Portland held a special place in her heart. It was the place where she could leave all of the negative things from her past behind, and become Kelsey North. There were too many reminders in Port Townsend for her to ever feel completely at peace there.

"What time is it?" Ryan asked.

"Four," Tyler replied.

"Excellent. Plenty of time," Ryan said.

"For what?" Jessica asked, dipping her spoon into Ryan's cup of ice cream.

"We have dinner plans," Ryan replied.

"We do?" Jessica asked.

"There a raw food restaurant near the condo. I want to go before it gets busy," Ryan said.

"Raw food?" Jessica asked.

"Mostly. It's supposed to be very good," Ryan said.

"It sounds healthy," Jessica said doubtfully.

"We like that sort of thing in the Pacific Northwest," Kelsey said.

"I know. You with your running and fit months," Jessica said.

"You take yoga," Kelsey pointed out.

"I know. I've been sucked into the granola lifestyle," Jessica said.

"You sound like Bob," Tyler said.

"I will eat vegetables," Jessica said.

"Yeah, Bob's ridiculous," Ryan commented.

"What's with that?" Jessica said. "It's like its a rule with him."

"Bob's family didn't have a lot of money when he was growing up. He said when he was an adult, he was going to eat meat at every meal. I think he's done just that," Ryan replied.

"Your spinach lasagna didn't have meat," Kelsey pointed out.

"I think Bob drove to McDonald's later that night. I heard the car after I went to bed," Ryan said.

"It's a half-hour drive from the campground," Kelsey said in disbelief.

"Okay, that's funny," Jessica laughed.

"It's an obsession," Ryan commented.

Once they finished their ice cream, they walked around Jamison Square Park. Then they continued their stroll through the Pearl District. Ryan bought Jessica a pair of silver earrings, and they took the streetcar for a few blocks.

"That was great!" Jessica said as they left it.

"We'll make sure we take it to Portland State," Kelsey said.

Around 6:30, Ryan led them to a yoga studio a couple of blocks from their condo.

"Yoga?" Jess asked, puzzled.

"We can come over for a class," Ryan said, but we're here for the food." He led them over to a counter and they looked at the menu.

"Healthy," Jessica said doubtfully.

"There's a McDonald's close by," Kelsey teased.

"Quiet," Ryan said to her. "What do you want Jess?"

"No clue. You order for me, I'll find a seat."

"Kels?" Ryan asked

"I'm with Jess. You guys pick something out," Kelsey said. She joined Jessica at a table.

"I'm so glad to be here with all of you," Jessica said, hanging her purse on the back of her chair.

"I'm glad you joined us."

"No, really. I don't know what I'd do if I was in New York. I guess I'd be sitting at home, having my father lecture me, and spend all of my time wondering if he was going to let me get on the plane to go back to Darrow," Jessica said.

"They really aren't going to pay for next year?"

"No way," Jessica said. "I guess I should thank Tyler and Ryan for wanting to pay for everything. Maybe I can save enough so I don't have to take out so many loans," she sighed.

Kelsey rubbed Jessica's arm in sympathy.

"It will work out," Kelsey said.

"It's nice of you to say so, Kels. But you've met my father. My not coming home for spring break was the ultimate betrayal."

"I'm sorry," Kelsey said sadly.

"Me, too," Jessica said. She looked up as Ryan and Tyler approached the table and sat down. "So what did you get for me?" she asked.

"You'll see. You'll like it," Ryan replied. Kelsey glanced at Tyler. His brown eyes were sparkling.

"Thank you for dinner," Kelsey said to him.

"You're welcome, Kelsey," Tyler replied.

Over the next hour, the group sampled chocolate-almond-butter smoothies, iced chai tea and Ryan's favorite — beet, cucumber, and celery juice. They ate bowls of brown rice smothered in warm greens, fresh vegetables, and delicious sauces. At the end of the meal, they split a coconut-chocolate nut bar.

"Okay, that was amazing," Jessica said, as they walked out onto the street.

"We should eat there every night," Ryan said.

"There's so many other great places. You'll miss out," Kelsey said.

"Fine. But we're definitely going back," Ryan said.

"I completely agree," Kelsey replied.

"Do you guys want to do yoga with us tomorrow?" Ryan asked them. He had picked up a yoga schedule on the way out.

"Kels?" Tyler asked doubtfully.

"No, thanks," Kelsey said.

"What's with you and yoga? It's like Bob with vegetables," Jessica said.

"I just don't find it relaxing. It's too slow," Kelsey said.

"That's the point," Jessica replied.

Tyler pulled out his smartphone and glanced at it. He put it back into his pocket.

"Let's go to Powell's," he said brightly.

"We just got here," Ryan said.

"So?" Tyler asked.

"You know you're going to want to go to that bookstore at least a dozen times on this vacation," Ryan said.

"And?" Tyler asked.

"Let's go to Powell's," Ryan said in defeat.

They walked over to Powell's Bookstore, a Portland institution.

"Wow," Jessica said, looking around.

"You'll want a map," Kelsey said, taking one from a display and handing it to Jessica.

"Are you kidding me?" Jessica said.

"It's a full city block," Kelsey said.

"Come on," Tyler said, with excitement.

"I want to go to cookbooks," Ryan said.

"I'll go with you," Jessica said.

"Message us then," Tyler said, pulling Kelsey's hand. She giggled. Tyler was like a kid in a candy store.

"Is there anywhere special you want to see?" he asked as they began to walk.

"I wouldn't mind seeing the health and fitness area," Kelsey said. "How about you?"

"I want to go to history and to languages," he said.

"Latin?" Kelsey asked.

"Norwegian. Margaret's got some good gossip lately, but my Norwegian ability isn't up to it."

Kelsey looked at him puzzled.

"Margaret only gossips about Lisa and Bob in Norwegian. Lisa doesn't speak it well," Tyler explained.

Kelsey laughed.

"So we're looking for a Norwegian/English gossip dictionary?"

"Exactly," Tyler replied.

About an hour and a half later, the couples met up. Both boys had fabric Powell's tote bags on their arms, full of books.

"Did you have fun? It looks like it," Tyler said to Ryan.

"I found two Ukrainian cookbooks. I'll practice so I can make something nice for Bob's birthday," Ryan said.

"Did you find anything, Jess?" Kelsey asked.

"Too much," Jessica said.

Ryan looked at his phone.

"Whole Foods closes in a half hour. I still want to go," he said.

"I'll drop the books at the condo and meet you over there," Tyler said. Ryan handed him the tote.

"I can go back with you," Kelsey said to Tyler. He shook his head.

"You're my chocolate advocate. Don't let Ryan make scones without it," Tyler said.

Ryan laughed and took Jessica's hand.

"It's not up to you," Ryan said.

"Says you," Tyler said. He kissed Kelsey. "See you in a minute," he said, and he left. Kelsey, Ryan, and Jessica headed out as well, and headed for the store. They passed by the cooking store, which was closed for the night.

"We can go tomorrow," Ryan said. Within three minutes of leaving the bookstore, they arrived at Whole Foods. Ryan got a cart.

"There's no way you're going to need that," Kelsey said.

"I want some snacks," Ryan said, wheeling the cart off.

"Give up, Kels," Jessica said. "You'll never rein Ryan in."

The girls followed Ryan back to the nut and dried fruit aisle. As Ryan was bagging hazelnuts, Kelsey looked up and saw Tyler stride into the aisle.

"Did he get my chocolate?" Tyler asked Kelsey, loudly enough for Ryan to hear.

"Not yet," Kelsey said.

"Not ever," Ryan retorted.

"You wish," Tyler grinned.

"Why don't you buy chocolate hazelnut spread?" Jessica suggested. "Then everyone's happy."

"Great idea. Come on, Kels," Tyler said, taking her hand. They walked to the jam aisle. As Kelsey was looking at the label on the chocolate hazelnut spread, Tyler pulled out his phone. Tyler looked at his phone, puzzlement on his face. He blinked, then bit his lip in thought. Kelsey saw him shrug gently, and place the phone back into his pocket.

"Do you care what kind we get?" she asked.

"Not as long as it's chocolate," Tyler replied. Kelsey pulled a jar off the shelf and they headed back to Ryan and Jess.

"Is that all you need?" Tyler asked. A large bag of hazelnuts sat alone in the cart. "Don't you need flour?"

"It's already in the condo. I ordered it ahead of time," Ryan said.

"What do you mean?" Jessica asked.

"What do you think the concierge is for? I sent over a shopping list," Ryan replied.

"This store is what, a block from the condo?" Jessica said.

"So?" Ryan said.

"Give up, Jessica," Kelsey said. Jessica giggled.

After adding a few snacks to the cart, they checked out and headed back to the condo.

"A fabulous day," Jessica said, sitting on the sofa.

"Very nice," Tyler agreed.

"I'm sitting on your bed," Jessica said to Tyler. "Are you going to sleep soon?"

Tyler shook his head. "I want to read my books," he replied.

"Learn some Norwegian," Kelsey teased.

"You know it, Princess," he said.

"I'm going to make the dough for the scones, then," Ryan said, walking into the kitchen.

"I'm going to put on my jammies," Jessica said.

"Nice," Ryan said.

"I meant sweats," Jessica said.

"Also nice," Ryan said. Jessica glared at him and left the room.

"You shouldn't tease her," Tyler said wisely. "She might decide not to live with us this summer."

"You don't think so?" Ryan said in panic.

"Jess is a good girl," Tyler said.

"Kelsey isn't," Ryan joked.

"Too bad you won't find out," Kelsey said. She opened the master bedroom door a small crack, saw that Jessica couldn't be seen, and walked into the room, closing the door behind herself. Jessica walked out of the master bathroom.

"We're locking the bedroom door," Jessica said, as she began braiding her hair.

"Ryan was kidding," Kelsey said.

"That's what you say," Jessica replied.

"Seriously, it was fine living with them last summer," Kelsey said. "They were perfect gentlemen."

"Maybe," Jessica said doubtfully. Kelsey opened her own bag and pulled out sweatpants and her pink Darrow t-shirt.

"I'll be back," Kelsey said, walking into the bathroom to change. When she returned a few minutes later, Jessica had finished braiding her hair, and was sitting on the king-sized bed, lost in thought.

"What's up?" Kelsey asked. She took a hair tie from her bag and put her hair into a ponytail.

"I'm just wondering what my father would say about this," Jessica said. She glanced up at Kelsey. "Living with boys." She laughed without mirth. "I'm sure he could come up with some choice names to call me."

"None of them would be true," Kelsey said. "People live together all the time and nothing happens."

"I know," Jessica sighed. "I just didn't grow up that way. I was raised believing that boys only wanted one thing, and nice girls made sure they didn't get it."

Kelsey laughed. "That's a lot of pressure."

"So you don't think this is wrong?"

"Living with those two?" Kelsey said. "No, I don't. Jess, my parents didn't think anything about me living with them last year."

"You said they let you do whatever you wanted to."

"They do, but they also know that just because a girl lives with a boy doesn't mean that something's going on," Kelsey replied.

"I guess. Nothing happened when we stayed with them last Easter or when I was with them at the Mercer," Jessica mused.

"Exactly. And nothing's going to happen this week or next summer. They just aren't like that."

"Ryan is."

"Ryan was, maybe," Kelsey gently corrected. "But he loves you. And he respects you."

"I guess," Jessica said.

"Jess, if you don't want to stay with them it's fine. We can get our own place this summer. We can get our own place now, here in Portland. I don't want you to feel uncomfortable," Kelsey said.

"Maybe I need to feel uncomfortable. Get out of my comfort zone," Jessica mused.

"Don't do anything you'll feel bad about later," Kelsey warned.

"I'm not doing anything with Ryan, if that's what you mean," Jessica said. "I'm just thinking that I should be willing to take more risks. Trusting myself a little more. Listening to my father a lot less." Jessica pulled gently on her braid. "Thanks, Kels. I appreciate your viewpoint. It's a real contrast to my own."

"Doesn't mean you're wrong."

"It doesn't mean I'm right either. Come on, let's go out," Jessica rose, and she and Kelsey left the bedroom.

Tyler glanced at Ryan.

"Sorry. I was just joking. You too, Kels," Ryan said.

"You don't bother me, Ryan," Kelsey said, sitting next to Tyler, who was reading his Norwegian book. Tyler put his arm around her and she leaned her head on his shoulder.

"It's okay," Jessica said. "How are the scones coming?"

"I just toasted the hazelnuts, so I'm waiting for them to cool," Ryan said.

Kelsey reached into the Powell's bag and pulled out her own book, a celebrity wellness guide. When she had looked at in in the store, she was surprised that it was actually well written and quite readable. She snuggled next to Tyler and read, as Jessica and Ryan puttered around in the kitchen.

Past midnight, everyone was still up. Ryan had finished the dough for the scones, which he would bake fresh tomorrow. He was making a shopping list from one of the recipes in his new Ukrainian cookbook. Jessica was lying on her stomach, engrossed in a novel. And Kelsey was looking through the fitness plan outlined in her book.

Tyler's phone buzzed, and he picked it up. Tyler looked at it. He sat quietly for a moment contemplating the message, Kelsey assumed, as she had looked up from her book to glance at him. A look of understanding came over his face and he smiled. He placed the phone back on the sofa next to himself.

"Good news?" Kelsey asked him curiously. Tyler had received a lot of messages today.

Tyler glanced at her. "For someone," he answered mysteriously.

The next morning, Kelsey and Tyler sat on the patio, fleece jackets over their sleepwear, eating warm chocolate-chip-hazelnut scones.

"Ryan actually put in chocolate," Kelsey said. Tyler smiled at her.

"I knew he would. He just needed a push," he said.

"If Bob won't eat sweets, he's really missing out. Ryan's great at baking."

"True, these are great. Thanks for reminding me," Tyler said, standing up abruptly. He walked back into the condo. He returned with his phone, and scrolled through the messages. He grinned, and placed the phone on the table.

Kelsey glanced at the phone, but all she saw were a series of messages with numbers.

N681RP outbound K0S9
N681RP inbound KVUO
N681RP outbound KVUO
N681RP inbound K0S9
N681RP outbound K0S9
N681RP inbound BUR
N681RP outbound BUR
N681RP inbound K0S9
N681RP outbound K0S9
N681RP inbound BFI

"You should probably call Morgan," Tyler said.

"Why?" Kelsey asked.

"No reason," Tyler said smiling and biting into his scone.

Jessica and Ryan returned a half hour later from their yoga class and had scones. Then everyone got dressed and they headed out.

"Where to today?" Jessica asked brightly. Kelsey smiled. Jessica was back in her element, feeling at home in a big city.

"I want to go to the cooking store," Ryan said.

"And the knitting store," Jessica added.

"Anywhere," Tyler said, holding Kelsey's hand, and looking at her.

"Then let's go," Kelsey said.

They began at the cooking store, which was kitty-corner from the condo. Ryan spent an hour and several hundred dollars there. He had everything shipped back to Seattle, and they continued their walk south.

The group's next stop was Jessica's knitting store, which didn't have the appropriate yarn for the charity baby hats, but did have a beautiful dark green wool and cashmere blend perfect for Ryan's next hat and scarf. Thrilled at Jessica's purchase and the promise of his new gift, Ryan kissed her outside of the store as he carried the paper bag full of yarn.

"Do you want another one?" Kelsey asked Tyler with trepidation. That hat and scarf had taken so much work, that she really wasn't sure she was up to making another one, particularly since she had also made a set for her father.

"The one I have is perfect. Thank you," Tyler replied, kissing her hair.

In the next two blocks, Kelsey took them all to a surprise. There was a lot with over sixty food trucks — the largest cluster of street food in America.

"I cannot believe we never knew about this." Tyler said to Ryan, biting into a Korean beef taco. Jessica had just gone off to get a plate of Pad Thai.

"I have to take notes," Ryan said. "After I eat, that is."

"You are the best girlfriend. Ever," Tyler said to Kelsey, after he finished chewing. Kelsey beamed.

They headed downtown on the streetcar, and ended up at Kelsey's alma mater, Portland State University.

"Ian will give us a tour next week when they're back in session." Kelsey said. "But I wanted to get a shirt at the bookstore."

"This is so cool," Jessica said, looking around at the urban campus. "I love how it's right in the city."

"Be careful, Jess," Kelsey said. The streetcar was heading on its route through campus.

"Wait, it goes right through the quad?" Jessica asked, as the streetcar passed them.

"Yep. You don't want to have your nose in a textbook when you're walking here," Kelsey commented. The group continued on into the bookstore.

Kelsey and Tyler headed for the campus clothing as Ryan and Jessica stopped at the magazines. Kelsey looked at the green and white shirts.

"What do you think?" Tyler asked from behind her. She turned. Tyler was holding up a dark green sweatshirt that read *Portland State*.

"Very nice," Kelsey said, smiling at him.

"I'll get it then," Tyler said, winking at her. "It's my girlfriend's alma mater."

Kelsey got a dark-green-and-white v-neck t-shirt, and white long-sleeved t-shirt, both with the same logo. Tyler wanted to pay, and she permitted him to do so. She kissed his cheek as he took the bag.

"Thank you very much, Tyler," Kelsey said.

"You're welcome, Princess," he replied.

After a brief — and this time, more careful — walk through the quad, they headed to downtown. They walked past the Hilton, went to a luxury department store, where Ryan insisted that Jessica buy a beautiful dress and the shoes to match, then they bought handcrafted chocolates at the mall. They ended their evening at a second-floor sushi restaurant in the Pearl.

Kelsey was putting on her new Portland State t-shirt when her phone rang. It was Jasmine. Kelsey picked up the phone. Ryan and Jessica were in the kitchen preparing biscuits for tomorrow's breakfast, and Tyler had gone across the street, back to Powell's Bookstore, to look at the Latin section.

"Hey, Jazz."

"Hey," Jasmine said. Jasmine didn't sound like her usual upbeat self. Kelsey wondered what was up.

"What's going on?" Kelsey asked.

"North, something interesting happened after you guys left," Jasmine said to her over the phone.

"Okay, what?"

"So everyone was talking about how you and your friends left on a private plane yesterday morning."

"I'm sure, because what else is there to discuss?" Kelsey commented.

"Well, the plane came back."

"Sure. Bob was still there."

"I'm not done, North," Jasmine warned.

"Sorry," Kelsey said, chagrined.

"Anyway, the plane came back and waited. Around dinnertime, a very familiar silver Honda parked at the airport, and Mr. Perkins and the driver left the car and got onto the plane. Jim checked online and said that the plane flew into Los Angeles."

"Los Angeles?" Kelsey asked. She thought Bob had returned to Seattle that night.

"Yep. It came back to Port Townsend again really late that night. The driver of the car got out alone, left with the car, and the plane flew to Seattle."

"And my hint is who drives a silver Honda," Kelsey said, but as soon as the words left her mouth, she knew. Morgan. "No way!" she said.

"She's not talking. Not a word. But I bet she'll tell you," Jasmine said.

"How did you find out?"

"Ben has a friend whose dad works at the airport. He mentioned it to Ben, because Ben overhears everything at Roxy's."

Kelsey thought back to Tyler's comments when Bob and Morgan went to the grocery store together for ice.

"I'll call her."

"Now," Jasmine said.

"Jazz. You cannot tell anyone. Let it die," Kelsey said.

"Why?"

"Because it's not nice to gossip about Morgan," Kelsey said. "Everyone else is okay."

Jasmine laughed. "You're right. We're like sisters. Fine. I won't even tell Jim. But find out what happened and tell her to tell me."

"Okay," Kelsey said. She disconnected with Jasmine, and called Morgan.

Morgan picked up on the first ring.

"Hey, Kels," Morgan said over the phone.

"Talk," Kelsey said.

"About what?" Morgan said innocently.

"Morgan."

"You won't tell anyone. Not a soul."

"No," Kelsey said.

"Okay, because I'm dying to tell someone. Wait a minute. I'll go outside," Morgan said, lowering her voice. Kelsey waited on hold and heard movement in the background.

"What does Jazz know?" Morgan asked a few moments later.

"That you and Bob Perkins took his plane to Los Angeles."

"She knows that much?" Morgan said in surprise.

"It's a small town, and a smaller airport," Kelsey said.

"How does she know we went to L.A.?" Morgan asked.

"Jim looked online. You can track private flights on the internet."

"Oh. I didn't know that," Morgan said thoughtfully.

"Stop stalling."

"All right, Kels. So you know I was having a conversation with Bob."

"Several," Kelsey said. In fact, Bob and Morgan had almost always been chatting with each other when they had been at the campground.

"He's nice to talk to. Anyway, I mentioned what Tyler had told us at Thanksgiving, about Bob using the plane to take people to dinner."

"Okay."

"So, he says, 'Do you want to go?' And I'm like, where? And he says, 'To dinner.' And I'm like, sure, I'm not going to pass up a free meal. So Bob asks me to pick him up at the campsite after you guys leave."

Morgan took a deep breath, and continued.

"So after work, I go to pick up Bob. I figure that he's going to take me into town, but he tells me to drive to the airport. And I'm wondering if we're going to eat there, but no, instead he tells me to park my car and we get on his plane, which is back from dropping you guys in Portland."

Kelsey shook her head as she listened to Morgan. She could tell from Morgan's voice this had been an experience of a lifetime.

"Kels. You know I'm freaking out right. I mean, we're getting on a plane? I've never been on a plane. But it was awesome."

Morgan continued, excitement in her voice. "We flew to Los Angeles, and there's a limousine waiting for us. And we get in, and Bob takes me for burgers." Morgan giggled. "Like you can't get a burger in Port Townsend. But it was great. Anyway, afterwards, he gives me a tour of L.A. I saw the Hollywood sign, we drove through Rodeo Drive and Beverly Hills, and we end up walking on the beach at Santa Monica. Then we drive back to the airport, fly back to Port Townsend, and Bob goes back to Seattle."

"He gave me his number, said I should call him and told me he'd take me to dinner again. Kelsey, what do I do?"

Kelsey sat on the bed in shock. It had taken her a long time to get used to the lifestyle that Tyler and Ryan lived. She could only imagine what Morgan had thought of all of this.

"Morgan, I have no idea," Kelsey said honestly. "Do you like him?"

"Bob's really nice."

"But he's older than your dad," Kelsey said.

"I know, but you know I like older guys," Morgan said.

"Morgan. Are you rationalizing this?" Kelsey asked her.

Morgan giggled. "Probably. It's not every day a guy flies you down the West Coast for a burger," Morgan said.

"True. Honestly, Morgan, I don't know what to tell you. You should do what you think is best," Kelsey said.

"Like I have a clue what that is," Morgan said.

"Why didn't you tell Jazz?"

"Because Jazz will tell everyone."

"Tell her. I told her not to blab," Kelsey said.

"Seriously?"

"She's on board. You can tell her," Kelsey said. "She'll help you think through it."

"I'm not sure there's anything to think about," Morgan said. "Bob's a nice guy and he's loaded. I'm not sure I can pass this up." Morgan paused. "Is this what being with Tyler is like?"

"Tyler hasn't flown me anywhere just for a burger," Kelsey said. "But he does live a very nice life."

"Kelsey, I never thought anything like that would happen to me," Morgan said.

Kelsey smiled, thinking of her own life with Tyler. "Yeah, me too," she agreed.

After Jessica and Ryan had each gone to bed so they could get up early for yoga class, Kelsey sat on the sofa with Tyler's arm around her.

"How did you know about Morgan?" Kelsey asked Tyler quietly.

"Know what?" Tyler asked innocently.

Kelsey glared at him. "Spill, Tyler Davis Olsen," she said.

Tyler grinned and pulled out his phone. He pulled up the messages Kelsey had seen before.

N681RP outbound K0S9
N681RP inbound KVUO
N681RP outbound KVUO
N681RP inbound K0S9
N681RP outbound K0S9
N681RP inbound BUR
N681RP outbound BUR
N681RP inbound K0S9
N681RP outbound K0S9
N681RP inbound BFI

"What is this? What does this mean?" Kelsey asked.

"Pull up Google on your phone," Tyler said. "I'm going to give you two clues and let you figure out the rest."

"What? Why?"

"Oh, come on. It will be fun. Morgan likes games, after all," Tyler said.

"Okay," Kelsey said. She pulled up Google.

"Ready?" Tyler asked.

"Yes," Kelsey said, a bit sullenly.

"You'll figure it out in a minute. You're quite smart, Miss North," Tyler said soothingly.

"Just give me my clues."

"All you have to do is type in the first or last letter-number combination of any line. One at a time," Tyler said.

"So, type in N681RP?" Kelsey asked.

"Right. Then hit search."

Kelsey did so. A bunch of aviation registrations came up. Tyler looked over her shoulder.

"Okay, another clue. Add the word Eclipse," Kelsey added it, then redid the search.

"See a name you recognize?"

Kelsey did. An Eclipse airplane with the registration of N681RP was registered to Robert Perkins.

"I guess the airplane registration number has been reused a few times," Tyler explained. "That's why you got the extra clue."

"So N681RP is Bob's plane. So what's K0S9?"

"Search and find out," Tyler said.

Kelsey cleared her search and typed in *K0S9*.

"Jefferson County International Airport?" Kelsey said. That was the name of Port Townsend's airport. Then she realized.

The beginning of each message was the same each time. Bob's plane registration.

The end of each message was an airport code.

Tyler had a list of all of the airports that Bob's plane had flown in and out of. She looked at the list again.

N681RP outbound K0S9

Bob's plane flew out of Port Townsend.

N681RP inbound KVUO

Kelsey typed KVUO into Google and hit search.

"Pearson Field, Vancouver, Washington," she read. Of course, Bob's plane had gone from Port Townsend to Vancouver. She had been on it.

N681RP outbound KVUO
N681RP inbound K0S9
N681RP outbound K0S9

Bob's plane had left Vancouver, Washington after dropping them off. It had flown back to Port Townsend, then left Port Townsend again. Kelsey assumed the plane had left Port Townsend with Bob, the only person left there. He was planning to fly back to Seattle that night.

N681RP inbound BUR
N681RP outbound BUR

Kelsey typed BUR into Google and hit search. Nothing of value came up.

"Try it with 'airport' added," Tyler said. Kelsey redid the search.

"Bob Hope Airport. Burbank, California. Los Angeles County," Kelsey read. Bob's plane had left Port Townsend, flown to Los Angeles, and left Los Angeles. She looked at the times. Every flight had been on Thursday night, the day they left.

N681RP inbound K0S9
N681RP outbound K0S9
N681RP inbound BFI

The plane flew into Port Townsend, left Port Townsend, and flew into BFI very early on Friday morning. Kelsey typed "BFI airport" into Google search.

"Boeing Field. King County International Airport. Seattle," Kelsey said. She looked up into Tyler's sparkling eyes.

"Did Bob mention going to Los Angeles to you?" Tyler asked Kelsey.

"No," Kelsey said. She understood now.

"And why would Bob's plane fly from L.A. to Port Townsend before it flew to Seattle? A little strange, right?" Tyler continued.

"A little," Kelsey said.

"Did Morgan confess?"

"My lips are sealed," Kelsey said.

"I bet they are," Tyler said. "Keep Morgan's secret. I know the truth."

The next morning, after Ryan and Jess returned from yoga and they all devoured Ryan's Southern style chicken and biscuits, Kelsey led them to the Portland Saturday Market.

"So why is it called the Saturday Market, when it's open on Saturday and Sunday?" Jessica asked.

"Because this is Portland," Kelsey answered.

"This is the cutest city," Jessica said happily.

They walked around the huge open-air craft market. Ryan bought Jessica a beautiful stone cuff bracelet, and Kelsey found a pair of earrings perfect for Jasmine. They stood in a twenty-minute line for some of the best donuts Kelsey had ever eaten, then the group split up. Ryan and Jessica headed back to the condo so Ryan could take Jessica and her new dress out to dinner.

Tyler and Kelsey walked along the waterfront. It had been drizzly all day, but neither of them were paying attention. They were too focused on each other.

"So what are you thinking about?" Kelsey asked Tyler.

"You," Tyler replied.

"What about me?" Kelsey asked.

"Everything," Tyler replied.

The next morning, Jessica left the condo early to go to Easter Mass at St. Andre's, and Tyler and Kelsey went running. They all arrived back at the condo, to discover that Ryan had prepared a sumptuous Easter brunch, complete with hot cross buns, dyed easter eggs and stuffed bunnies for the girls, and a giant chocolate bunny for Tyler.

They spent a quiet Easter Sunday together, returning to Jamison Square Park, then walking up to Tanner Springs Park to see the art wall and walk through the wetlands. They ended up on the playground at the Fields Neighborhood Park, where Ryan and Jessica played a game of tag with a pair of five-year-old twins in their Easter dresses, while their tired, grateful parents watched.

On Monday, the group split up again. Ryan and Jessica went back downtown to shop, while Kelsey and Tyler hung around the Pearl. As they were heading back through the grassy North Park Blocks to meet Ryan and Jessica for their second dinner at the raw food restaurant, Tyler lifted Kelsey's hand and kissed it.

"Are you having a good vacation, Princess?" he asked.

"I am," Kelsey replied. "Are you?"

"Very much. I'm dreading going back."

Kelsey smiled. Tyler had got a message this morning with the list of the four first-year law students who would be joining him and the others on Law Review. A reminder of what awaited him upon his return.

"But," he continued, "we'll still be together. And that makes all the difference to me."

"Me, too," Kelsey agreed. They stopped on the sidewalk in front of the Customs House. She looked at Tyler, and he smiled at her.

"I love you so much," he said softly. "I can't believe you're mine."

"All you had to do was ask," Kelsey said, taking his face in her hands and kissing him.

The next afternoon, the group took the elevator down to the garage. They had yet to use the car, but today was the day. Jessica and Kelsey would be meeting up with Dylan for the first time in months, and he had requested that they meet him over in the Hawthorne District. They walked over to parking space A-2, where a sleek black Porsche 911 awaited them.

"Of course Bob wouldn't have a Kia," Jessica said, lifting an eyebrow.

"This is beautiful," Kelsey said, looking at it. She wondered what Morgan, who loved sports cars, would say.

"Not much room in the back, though," Jessica commented.

"I'd offer to sit there, but I'm driving," Tyler said.

"You're driving?" Ryan said.

"Of course."

"It's my father's car."

"All the more reason he'd want me to drive it. Get in," Tyler replied. Ryan frowned, but held the seat for the girls as they climbed in.

"It's more comfy than I thought," Jessica said to Kelsey as she put on her seat belt. Kelsey agreed. In the driver's seat, Tyler took off his new Portland State sweatshirt and tossed it in Ryan's lap.

"Hang on to that for me, please," he said. He started the engine and they drove off.

Kelsey looked out of the window as they drove across Portland. Tyler took the route over the Morrison Bridge, and less than 15 minutes from when they left the condo, they arrived at the cafe where they were supposed to meet Dylan.

"So when should we pick you up?" Tyler asked as the girls climbed out of the car. Kelsey looked around. It didn't look like Dylan had arrived yet.

"Two hours?" Kelsey said.

"We'll be back in an hour and a half. You won't be able to tolerate Dylan for that long," Tyler said.

Kelsey giggled, but Jessica looked confused. Kelsey had only given Jessica a brief overview of her disastrous Thanksgiving with Dylan.

"See you in ninety minutes," Tyler said, giving Kelsey a kiss. Ryan kissed Jessica on the cheek and the boys left.

"Let's get a seat," Jessica said brightly. "I'm so excited to see Dylan."

Kelsey was a little less excited. After Thanksgiving, she wanted to know if this was one of Dylan's good days, or one of the bad. Maybe she should have called Dylan's brother Ian this morning to get the report on Dylan's mood.

The girls sat and ordered coffee. Dylan Shaw strolled in a few minutes later.

"Dylan!" Jessica squealed. Kelsey laughed. Jessica had always loved Dylan. Jess stood up and gave him a hug.

"It's great to see you, Jess," he said, hugging her back. "Hi, Kels," he said, sitting next to her.

"Nice to see you."

"I'm glad you two could come to my hometown," Dylan said, signaling to the waiter. "Caramel latte and a Nanaimo bar," he said when the waiter arrived.

"Two Nanaimo bars," Kelsey corrected. The waiter nodded and walked off.

"What's a Nanaimo bar?" Jessica asked.

"Heaven," Kelsey said.

"I thought you called yourself a Seattleite, Jess," Dylan grinned.

"New Yorker, through and through," Jessica replied.

Jessica and Dylan, who hadn't seen each other for over a year, immediately launched into a conversation, which moved from things that had happened at Darrow since Dylan had left, to Dylan's somber recollection of his stint in rehab and subsequent return to Portland. They also had a long discussion of cool things to do on the girls' final days in the Rose City.

Kelsey was beginning to breathe a sigh of relief. Maybe the old Dylan was back.

After the consumption of the coffees and Nanaimo bars — sweet, delicious dessert bars covered with icing and a layer of chocolate — the talk turned to future plans.

"So where are you going to school?" Jessica asked Dylan.

"Lewis and Clark," Dylan replied.

"Congratulations," Kelsey said to him.

"It's here in Portland?" Jessica asked.

"Yes," Dylan said.

"You don't want to come back to Seattle? Be with us?" Jessica asked.

Dylan looked at Kelsey meaningfully. "Someone doesn't want me there," he said.

Kelsey sighed quietly. It looked like this was going to be a bad day with Dylan after all. So much for being hopeful.

She glanced at her phone. At least the boys should be back soon.

"I didn't say that," Kelsey replied.

"No? What did you say?" Dylan asked.

"I said I wasn't dating you," Kelsey said.

"Why would you? You're dating Tyler," Jessica interjected.

Dylan looked at Kelsey. "Well, when did this happen, Miss North?"

"When we got back to school after Thanksgiving," she replied.

"He couldn't bear the thought of someone snatching you up?" Dylan asked.

"Drop it, Dylan," Kelsey said.

Jessica looked from one to the other. "What's going on?" she asked.

"Kelsey wouldn't go out with me," Dylan said.

"You asked her? He asked you?" Jessica said.

"He wasn't serious," Kelsey replied, glaring at Dylan.

"I was as serious as a heart attack," Dylan replied.

"Do we really have to discuss this again?" Kelsey said in exasperation.

"No."

"Good."

"So what's it like dating a billionaire? Has he showered you with diamonds yet?" Dylan asked.

"So funny."

"What's with you?" Jessica asked Dylan.

"I should ask you the same question. Are you really going out with Ryan Perkins?" Dylan confronted Jessica.

"I am," Jessica said, in a no-nonsense tone.

"I would have expected better of you," Dylan said.

"What does that mean?" Jessica asked.

"You're kidding, right?" Dylan said to her.

"No, I'm not," Jessica replied.

"Jess, Ryan Perkins is an idiot. Everyone knows that."

"Does everyone? Because he's doing pretty well at Darrow."

"He must be paying someone off. He's certainly got enough money," Dylan said.

"Ryan's still at Darrow, unlike some people I know," Jessica replied.

Dylan narrowed his eyes at Jessica. Kelsey slipped down in her chair. She wanted to be anywhere but here right now.

"Perhaps he's managed to keep his drug addiction under control," Dylan replied.

"Ryan doesn't do drugs!" Jessica said in outrage.

"That's why he's got a conviction for possession," Dylan replied. "Maybe you're the idiot."

"How dare you?" Jessica said, standing up. Kelsey looked out of the front window, and breathed a sigh of relief. Tyler was parking the car outside of the cafe. "You don't know anything about me or about Ryan. What did I ever see in you?"

"I don't know. I never saw anything in you," Dylan said.

"Dylan!" Kelsey said. She couldn't believe what she had just heard. Tyler, wearing his Portland State shirt, and Ryan, carrying a trio of roses for Jessica, walked into the cafe door.

"Oh, yay," Dylan said.

"Nice to see you too, Mr. Shaw," Tyler said, sitting in one of the two now-empty chairs at the table.

"We were just leaving," Jessica said sharply.

"Okay," Ryan said, confused.

"Are you enjoying your purchase, Mr. Perkins?" Dylan asked.

"What?" Ryan asked.

"I bet Miss Hunter is very expensive. How much did you pay for her to be your girlfriend?" Dylan asked.

"Jessica loves me," Ryan said.

"Of course I do. We're leaving," Jessica snapped, standing up and glaring at Dylan. She took Ryan's hand and walked out of the cafe with him.

"Making friends everywhere," Tyler quipped.

"Shut up, Olsen," Dylan said.

"Have you been dealing with this for an hour and a half?" Tyler asked Kelsey.

She shook her head. Kelsey looked at Dylan. "What is wrong with you? Really, I don't get it," she said.

Dylan ignored her. "Why are you wearing that?" he asked Tyler.

"Wearing what?"

"A Portland State shirt. You didn't go to Portland State."

"So?"

"So you shouldn't be wearing it."

"Dylan, really? Tyler, let's go," Kelsey said. "Dylan's decided to be insane." Kelsey stood, but Tyler remained in his chair, looking at Dylan.

"Why not?" Tyler asked.

Dylan pondered Tyler.

"Is this some kind of joke to you? Billionaire meets small-town girl and goes slumming. What happens to Kelsey when you get bored and marry a socialite, Tyler?"

"Wow," Tyler said. "I didn't realize that you had such a low opinion of Kelsey," he said.

"Yeah, me neither," Kelsey said. "Tyler, let's go."

Dylan looked at her. He looked surprised at his own words. "I didn't mean it like that, Kels," he backpedaled.

"I don't care what you meant it like, Dylan. Goodbye," Tyler stood up, and Kelsey took his hand. They left the cafe. Ryan was sitting in the backseat of the car holding Jessica, who was crying.

"Jess, what's wrong?" Kelsey asked. But Jessica didn't answer.

They returned to the condo. Jessica went into the master bedroom without a word and shut the door.

"Well, that was a nightmare. Again," Tyler said to Kelsey.

"I'm sorry. Both of you. I was hoping he had gotten that out of his system last Thanksgiving."

"Why is Jess so upset?" Ryan asked in worry. "What did he say to her?"

"I don't know," Kelsey said. She had been wondering the same thing. Jessica had been angry, not upset, when she had left the table. "I'll talk to her," she said soothingly to Ryan.

"It's okay. Kelsey knows how to cheer up Jess," Tyler said to Ryan. "Why don't you bake some cookies? Chocolate chip."

Ryan laughed. "For you?"

"Sure, why not? I was traumatized too," Tyler said. Kelsey gave him a kiss. She walked over to the master bedroom door, and knocked gently. Then she let herself in.

Jessica was sitting on the bed. A mound of crumpled tissues sat next to her. She was wiping her eyes as Kelsey put her arm around her shoulders.

"Dylan's a jerk," Kelsey said.

"I know," Jessica sniffled. "I'm not crying over Dylan," she said.

"Why are you crying?" Kelsey asked.

"I'm tired, Kels. I'm tired of explaining Ryan. Of justifying why I'm going out with him. Of fighting against his past. I just don't know how much longer I can do this," Jessica said.

Kelsey nodded. "Then stop," she said.

Jessica looked up at her in surprise. "Break up with him?" she asked.

"No. Stop explaining. No one deserves an explanation. It's nobody's business, except yours and Ryan's. You don't have to justify anything, to anybody."

Jessica looked at Kelsey, dumbfounded. "You really believe that?"

"Of course I do. Jessica, you have to live your life for yourself. All these people who are questioning you, criticizing what you do, where will they be in five years? In twenty? Will they be there supporting you, or will they find new things to complain about? You will never, ever make everyone happy. So focus on the one person who can make you happy. You."

Kelsey rubbed Jessica's back gently.

"Jess, other people will run your life into the ground if you let them. Even people who claim that they care about you. Everyone has their own agenda, and despite what they say, it isn't always in your best interest to take their advice. Do you love Ryan?"

"More than anyone," Jessica said softly.

"Then you know what to do," Kelsey replied.

"Is she okay?" Ryan asked as Kelsey walked out of the bedroom fifteen minutes later.

"She's fine. She'll be out in a minute." Kelsey sat next to Tyler, who was picking up a hot, gooey chocolate chip cookie off a plate in front of him.

"Ryan made you cookies?" Kelsey asked. "You really are spoiled."

Tyler grinned and placed a piece of the hot cookie into his mouth. Jessica walked into the room and Ryan ran over to her and gave her a hug.

"Are you okay, Jess?" he asked in concern.

Jessica closed her eyes and pulled Ryan closer. "I've never been better," she replied.

As the girls joined them for cookies, the boys confessed where they had gone. Bob had recently met an executive at Nike, and to the executive's vast amusement, Bob had requested passes to the Nike employee store, where everything was a minimum of 50% off. Bob had given the passes to Ryan, with the request that Ryan buy him running shoes.

Despite the girls' agreement to allow them to buy things over the vacation, the boys decided to go to the store alone and buy gifts for Kelsey and Jess.

"Seriously? You two haven't done enough?" Kelsey asked.

"Nope," Ryan said. "I'll go get the bags."

Ryan left the condo, while Jessica took a cookie from the plate. Kelsey eyed Tyler, who spoke.

"Dave Jensen is in no danger of getting a gift from Miss Hunter, who's been quite diligent thanks to letting Ryan buy her a dress, but you..." Tyler shook his head mournfully.

"What? I've been following your rules," Kelsey retorted.

"You didn't let me pay for your earrings," Tyler said.

"They are a gift for Jasmine," Kelsey explained.

Tyler shrugged. "I did what I could, but there was a lot of bright pink at the Nike store and I know how you feel about that. At the rate you're going, Professor Eliot can expect a 'World's Greatest Professor' mug from you at a bare minimum."

Kelsey thought for a moment. "Let's go out," she finally said.

"Now?" Tyler asked.

"The stores are open until nine. We're finishing this today," Kelsey said.

"Okay," Tyler grinned. "Jess, can you guys text us when you're ready for dinner, and we'll meet you?"

"You can, but I'm not eating until we're done," Kelsey replied.

"I'll let him know. You can do it, Kels," Jessica said.

Kelsey got her fleece jacket and she and Tyler headed out. The elevator doors opened and Ryan stepped out, arms full of Nike bags.

"Where are you going?" he asked.

"Jess will explain," Tyler replied. He and Kelsey got on the elevator and Tyler pressed the button for the lobby.

"How much do I have to spend?" Kelsey asked him.

"A lot."

"Why are you doing this?"

"I don't want you to deny yourself anything," Tyler replied, as the elevator doors opened. They walked out into the lobby, then out onto the street.

"I'm not," Kelsey said.

"Kelsey, you pick up things. You look at something, think for a moment, put it back on the shelf, then pick it up again, then put it back again. It makes me crazy," Tyler said, taking her hand.

"Why?"

"Because you can have anything you want."

"Suppose I don't want anything?" Kelsey asked.

"Of course you want things," Tyler replied.

"Sure, some things. But not everything," Kelsey said.

"But you won't let me get you anything," Tyler said. "Even Jess lets Ryan buy things for her sometimes."

Kelsey thought for a moment as they headed down the street. She stopped on the corner.

"When you buy me something, what does that mean to you?" Kelsey asked.

"What does it mean to me?" Tyler asked.

"How do you feel?"

"Like I'm taking care of you," he replied.

"Why?"

"Because, when I was growing up, I never had a lot of time with my mother. But I knew that she worked hard and provided me with everything I could possibly need or want. That's how I knew she loved me."

"But I know you love me. Even when you don't give me anything at all," Kelsey said.

Tyler looked at her.

"Maybe you equate things with love because that's what you were provided with as a child. But what I treasure is your time. There's nothing more I need from you," Kelsey continued.

"Are you my therapist?"

Kelsey smiled. "Maybe. Tyler, I love you. Your intellect, your kindness. My favorite times on this vacation have been when it's just you and me, holding hands, and being together. In the forest, on the waterfront, when you have nothing to do and nowhere to be. That's what I love."

Tyler frowned. "But it will end. That's what scares me. We'll graduate, I'll go work for Tactec, and I'll be just like my Mom and Bob. I won't have time for you any more. So how can I show you that I love you, except by giving you things?" he asked.

Kelsey looked at him in concern. She could hear the uncertainty in his voice.

"If I show you now that money means love, you'll never wonder if I love you," he said softly. "Because I'll always have money. But I won't always have time."

Kelsey felt tears spring to her eyes.

"Is this what this is about? Are you afraid that I won't know that you love me?" she asked.

Tyler nodded sadly.

"I thought you were smart," Kelsey said with as much sarcasm as she could muster and sniffling the tears away. But Tyler wasn't fooled.

"Kelsey, do you know why Chris thought my mother was having an affair with Bob? It was because she was always at the office. 365 days a year, seven days a week. What happens when I'm doing what she did? Missing Christmas and birthdays? Will you doubt me too?"

"Never," Kelsey said seriously. "I know what I'm in for. Chris didn't. I'll understand."

"Are you sure? Because a lot of people don't. Simon's been divorced too."

"Tyler, I will always know that when you aren't with me, you want to be with me. I know that clearly. You don't need to prove anything to me. And you certainly don't need to spend money on me to show me that you love me."

"You say that," Tyler said. "But what happens when I'm working eighteen-hour days?"

"Will you come home to me?"

"Yes."

"Then I will know that you love me. Tyler, when I was younger, our store wasn't doing well for a while. My father worked nonstop to make things better, but my mother thought that his being away from her meant he didn't love her. I thought so too. It took me a long time to realize that his working so hard was his way of showing his love for us. I won't make that mistake again.

"He was sacrificing what he wanted most, time with his family, to give us the life he wanted us to have. You'll do the same, to make sure that your children and grandchildren have better lives."

"So they can grow up like Ryan and spend their lives destroying expensive cars and dating supermodels?" Tyler asked wryly.

"Okay, the analogy doesn't hold perfectly," Kelsey smiled. "But you see my point."

"I do."

"Do you know what I thought when I didn't see you during the last couple of weeks of Law Review?" Kelsey asked.

Tyler shook his head.

"I was proud of you. You had promised to work hard on something, and that's exactly what you did. I'll feel the same way this summer when you're working for Simon. I know how limited your time is, and that's why I'm so happy when you choose to share it with me. Whether it's a day or an hour, I know that you're taking the thing that is most valuable to you, time, and giving it to me. Money is meaningless to you."

"It isn't meaningless to you," Tyler pointed out.

"The money I earn isn't. But yours is."

Tyler sighed.

"So I can't buy your love?"

"You've earned my love," Kelsey said. "It's yours, for as long as you want it."

"Suppose I want it forever?"

"Then it's yours forever," Kelsey replied.

"I thought you were going to make Kelsey buy a bunch of stuff." Ryan said, as Tyler and Kelsey sat down at the table for dinner. They had joined Ryan and Jessica at a wood-fired pizza restaurant steps from the condo. Tyler smiled at Kelsey.

"Don't worry, Kelsey made me pay," he said.

"So what did you get?" Jessica asked her.

"Something very expensive," Kelsey replied, winking at Tyler.

The next day, Tyler drove Kelsey to Forest Park so they could take a long walk in the woods. Per yesterday's agreement with Kelsey, he was required to spend at least ten hours alone with her before their vacation was over. In exchange for giving her his time, he would drop his requirement that she spend his money. Professor Eliot would not be getting a gift this year.

"You certainly have a way with Miss Hunter. She's in a much better mood," Tyler commented as they walked.

It was true. Every since their lunch with Dylan, Jessica had seemed much more upbeat and happy. She seemed to have taken Kelsey's words to heart, or at least, given them some thought.

During what Jessica had termed her 'therapy session', she had confided in Kelsey her deep love for her father, and her willingness to bend to his will to make sure that he continued to love her too.

Jess had always felt that his love for her was conditional on her adherence to his rules.

One of the things that had attracted her to Ryan, Jessica admitted, was his unconditional love for her. No matter what she had said, Ryan remained by her side and over the time they had spent together, Jessica was finally beginning to believe that he always would.

On Thursday, they met Ian, Dylan's younger brother, for a tour of Portland State University. The boys were wary, until Kelsey explained that not only was Ian the exact opposite of Dylan, Dylan was usually angry with Ian as well. They met Ian not on the downtown campus, but at the new Life Sciences building, a ten-minute streetcar ride away.

"So this is where Biology classes are held now?" Tyler asked looking around in interest.

"Yep," Ian said, as they walked through the beautiful building, which was filled with natural light.

"I just missed it," Kelsey said, interested as well. The building had opened as she had arrived at Darrow.

"We share it with Oregon State and OSHU," Ian commented.

"I bet the labs are amazing," Kelsey said.

"They're great," Ian said. Ian, to everyone's surprise, including his own, was planning on becoming a chemistry major, which also had its classes and labs in the building.

"Kelsey North?" a voice called. Kelsey turned around.

"Professor Barrow!" Kelsey said happily. She walked over to him and shook his hand.

"Taking the tour?" he asked.

"I am. Have you met Ian Shaw?"

"I haven't. Nice to meet you," Professor Barrow said, shaking Ian's hand.

"And these are my friends from Darrow Law School," Kelsey added. Professor Barrow greeted them, then shook his head.

"I'm still not over the fact that you went to law school instead of going for your Ph.D," he commented.

"I'm still thinking about it," Kelsey said.

"I hope so," Professor Barrow said. "It was nice to meet you all. Kelsey, keep in touch. And if you decide to apply to grad school, I'm happy to write your recommendation."

"Thanks, Professor," Kelsey said. Professor Barrow waved, and headed down the hall.

"You're friends with Barrow?" Ian said.

"He's a great professor," Kelsey said.

"I've heard he's a really tough grader."

Kelsey thought for a moment. "Yeah, I heard that too," she replied.

"You do get along with everyone," Ian commented.

"Except your brother," Kelsey said wryly.

Ian laughed. "I wouldn't know. Dylan's not speaking to me either."

"Why?" Kelsey asked. It wasn't uncommon for Dylan to be angry with Ian, but there was usually an amusing reason why.

"I dented his car."

"Again?"

"It wasn't my fault," Ian said.

"It never is," Kelsey teased.

"No, really this time, it wasn't. I borrowed his car to run to Fred Meyer, and when I came out, there was a big dent. I think one of the shopping carts ran into it," Ian said.

Kelsey giggled. "Why did you borrow his car?"

Ian looked sheepish. "Mine was in the shop."

"Because?" Ian wasn't the most responsible person on earth.

"I forgot to put oil in it," Ian said.

“Oh, Ian,” Kelsey laughed.

“I know, I’m hopeless right, Kels?” Ian said.

“No, you’re Ian,” Kelsey said with a grin.

Friday, Kelsey woke up to her phone vibrating. She looked at the readout, and sighed inwardly. It was Dylan. She was tempted to ignore it, but she decided that she would need to talk to him at some point, and it might as well be now. She slipped out of the covers and took the phone into the master bathroom. She closed the door.

“Hello?” she said quietly, so as not to wake Jessica, who was still fast asleep.

“Kels,” Dylan replied. Kelsey could hear the hesitation in his voice. “I’m sorry.”

“Okay,” Kelsey replied.

Dylan sighed. “You know I think the world of your family,” he said.

“I know,” Kelsey said. Dylan was silent for a moment, but Kelsey didn’t feel the need to fill the air. This was Dylan’s call.

“I hate that you’re going out with Tyler,” he said.

“I got that,” Kelsey replied. “Why?”

“Because I know that he loves you,” Dylan replied. “And I’m jealous because I love you too.”

“You don’t love me like that.”

“No. You’re right. I’m jealous because he has the kind of relationship I want. And it’s not fair because he has everything else too.”

"He doesn't."

"You say that, Kels. But he has money, he's at the top of his class at Darrow, and he's got probably the best girlfriend on the planet."

"You'll find your girl," Kelsey said.

"I know. And I have money. But I'll never get Darrow back."

"No."

"I mean, Ryan Perkins has managed to stay? I feel like such a loser," Dylan commented.

"He's got the right motivation," Kelsey replied.

"Jess?"

"Yeah," Kelsey said.

"What happened to her?"

"Nothing. Something happened to you," Kelsey commented.

"Maybe," Dylan conceded. He sighed. "How's Ian?"

"Good. You haven't spoken to your own brother lately?" Kelsey asked, amused.

"I try not to. I'm always yelling at him."

"You seem to always be yelling at everyone," Kelsey said.

"I have a lot of anger."

"You didn't use to," Kelsey said.

"I'm not dealing with this well, Kelsey."

"I can tell," Kelsey replied. "But you need to do better."

"I know," Dylan said. "Are you having a good vacation?"

"I am."

"Does he treat you well?" Dylan asked her.

"He does."

"I figured he would," Dylan said. He sighed. "I'm so sorry, Kelsey. I'm failing as your friend."

"We all have good and bad days, Dylan."

"I always seem to see you on the bad ones," Dylan replied.

"That does seem to be true."

"Enjoy the rest of your break and good luck with Darrow."

"Thanks," Kelsey said.

"Bye," Dylan said.

"Goodbye, Dylan," Kelsey said. And she hung up.

After everyone else in the condo awoke, they ate a late breakfast and headed to OMSI, the Oregon Museum of Science and Industry. Everyone loved the science museum, and they weren't surprised that they managed to spend almost the entire day playing in the exhibits.

After the museum, they split up. Ryan and Jessica went off to a gourmet meal in an artisan restaurant, while Kelsey and Tyler went to another brewpub for burgers.

"Are you sure you don't want to eat somewhere else?" Tyler asked, glancing at Kelsey behind his menu.

"I know you can afford better, Tyler, but this is fine."

Tyler grinned at her, and looked back at his menu. "Thanks," he said. "I get tired of the pretentious restaurant scene."

"Sometimes you just want a burger and fries," Kelsey agreed.

They placed their orders and their drinks arrived. Kelsey stirred her chocolate milkshake with a straw.

"Dylan called me this morning," she said.

"Did he?" Tyler replied. "What did Mr. Shaw say?"

"He apologized," she replied.

"He needed to," Tyler said. Kelsey nodded.

It was interesting to Kelsey how little Dylan knew about Tyler. His comment about Tyler slumming had almost made her laugh.

Kelsey knew better than anyone that if she offered to trade her normal middle-class family for Tyler's, he'd take her up on the offer and throw in his two billion dollars as a sweetener for the deal. Kelsey and Tyler hadn't even discussed Dylan's accusation, because it was so unbelievable.

"So you liked the museum? What was your favorite part?" Kelsey asked him.

"The submarine, obviously," Tyler replied. OSMI was known for having an actual submarine anchored on the river which you could tour. Their tour guide had actually served on board a submarine, and was full of interesting tales from his experience.

"Yeah, that was so cool," Kelsey agreed. "I could never do that," she said.

"Do what?"

"Live on a submarine," she replied.

"You'd have to have a really strong mindset to be able to do that. Frankly, I think that's true for everyone who joins the military," Tyler commented.

Kelsey giggled. "First of all, you have to get up early," she said, looking at Tyler.

"That wouldn't work too well for me," Tyler conceded.

"I'm thinking that," Kelsey said. "You have a lot of discipline though, you could make it work."

"I'd rather not find out," Tyler said.

"My friend Matt's in the service. He's the only person I know who's as disciplined as you," Kelsey said.

"You mean besides you," Tyler said.

"Maybe," Kelsey agreed. The waitress arrived with a plate of waffle fries, and a side of fried mozzarella sticks. She left, and Kelsey took a mozzarella stick.

"I'm going to be in real trouble when I get measured for my bridesmaid dress."

"Skipping your fit month?"

"Yeah, Jasmine wasn't happy, but I told her I wasn't giving up the chance to eat in Portland. Maybe I'll do it in October."

"Should we get the personal trainer back?" Tyler asked.

"Maybe," Kelsey said.

"Only if you wake me up for every workout again," Tyler said, eyes sparkling. Kelsey blushed at the thought.

Saturday morning, Ryan made another special brunch for the group. It was their last full day in Portland, and everyone had something that they wanted to return to. Ryan began by heading back to the cooking store, where he bought more things to be shipped back to Seattle. Jessica led the group back to the Saturday market, and Kelsey took them all on another walk on the waterfront.

Tyler, of course, wanted to go back to Powell's Bookstore. Kelsey had lost track of how many times he had gone, since more than once he had run over late at night or first thing in the morning, thanks to it being across the street from the condo. They ended their night at the raw food restaurant, where Ryan asked lots of questions. The other three knew they could look forward to great meals to come.

After brunch in the Pearl District on Sunday, everyone packed their bags. Ryan had dropped a large box off with the concierge to be shipped to Bob, which contained six pairs of running shoes. A second large box would be shipped to Darrow, full of the books Tyler had bought. The other purchases they had made went into a third box, to join them on the flight back.

Once they had packed, they headed downstairs, said goodbye to the concierge and walked out to the waiting limousine. As the driver placed their packages in the trunk, Jessica looked around happily with Ryan's arm around her shoulders.

"I can't wait to come back," she said. "Thanks, you guys."

They were driven to the airport in Vancouver, Washington, where once again, Captain McAdams was waiting for them. This time, Kelsey noticed the registration painted clearly the tail of the plane, N681RP. They returned to their seats as before, only this time, Jessica and Kelsey didn't squeeze each other's hands quite as tightly. Captain McAdams expertly flew them back across Western Washington, and a few moments after they all looked in amazement at the majesty that was Mount Rainier, he guided them safely down to the runway at Boeing Field.

The next morning, Kelsey met Tyler in the gym. She was wearing one of her many presents from the Nike store, a black-and-lilac tank and short set, with matching running shoes.

Tyler surveyed her slowly with his eyes. A sexy grin spread across his face.

"Now I'm awake," he commented. And he kissed her.

She met Tyler and Ryan for breakfast an hour and a half later, and they all headed over to their new intellectual property class, Patents. Once they arrived in the classroom, they greeted their fellow IP classmates, who they had got to know quite well over the past year, and found seats together. A few moments later, Professor Lila Schwartz walked in, and class began.

"Someone's in trouble," Tyler said, looking at Ryan at lunch.

"I don't know why Professor Schwartz thinks that I know anything about patents," Ryan groused. Professor Schwartz had called Ryan out in class about the Tactec patents and Ryan had stumbled through an answer.

"Oh, I don't know. Because your father's company holds thousands of them," Tyler replied.

"I spent my time at Tactec working on litigation, not patents," Ryan said.

"Too bad for you," Tyler said.

"I'll have to talk to Lisa," Ryan said. "She'll help me."

"Better do it quick. Professor Schwartz looked like she had more to say, and we have class on Wednesday," Tyler commented.

Ryan sighed. "Where is Lisa?" he asked Tyler. Tyler thought for a moment.

"Bellevue, I think."

"Not traveling?" Jessica asked. Tyler shook his head.

"I'll call her," Ryan said, picking up his phone and walking away from the table. Kelsey watched him.

"Does your mother really do his homework?" Kelsey asked Tyler.

"I wouldn't be surprised," Tyler commented.

Kelsey and Jessica returned from picking up their grades. Kelsey had got As in all of her classes, including Professor Bell's. She still felt a little guilt about the exam, although she knew Tyler didn't. Jessica had got two Bs and a C once again in tax.

"So frustrating," Jessica said about her tax grade, placing her grades and phone on the coffee table. Suddenly, the phone rang, and Jessica slid her finger across the screen to answer it. She put it on speaker.

"Andrea," Jessica answered.

"Hey, sweetie," Andrea said to Jessica.

"Hi. How's it going?"

"Not good, but I know you know that," Andrea replied.

"What happened?"

"Your father could not believe that you didn't come back for Spring Break."

"I'm not coming back this summer either. I have a job here," Jessica said defiantly.

"Jess, you know that I love you, but I think you're playing with fire," Andrea said.

"What do you mean?"

"I mean, your father isn't going to tolerate this. His brothers and yours are telling him he needs to force you to return."

"How? Drag me onto a plane?"

"Cut you out of the family," Andrea said. "Let you beg your way back in."

"I'm not part of the family. I'm chattel. An object my father can order about," Jessica said.

Andrea sighed.

"I don't disagree, but there are going to be consequences for you."

"I'll accept them. I have to live my own life, Andrea."

"I know. Joey says you're hardheaded. That's one of the things I've always loved about you."

"Thanks," Jessica said.

"Jessie, think about it. I know that you want to stay at Darrow and with your boyfriend, but your father's going to make sure there's a steep price to pay."

"Yeah," Jessica sighed. "But there's no compromise with him. It's his way, or the highway. This time, I'm going to choose the highway."

Tyler had been forced to miss his usual Friday date with Kelsey due to a Law Review meeting, so he had promised to make it up to her on Saturday afternoon.

"So where are we going?" Kelsey asked him.

"It's a surprise," Tyler said. He was driving his car, and Kelsey hadn't been told to get dressed in anything other than fleece, so she was very curious. They were heading downtown.

"You and your surprises," Kelsey teased.

"You don't like them?" Tyler asked.

"I love them. But I know how busy you are," Kelsey said.

"This didn't take any time to plan," Tyler said. "I remember Papa Jefferson's maxim. Moderation."

"Okay," Kelsey said.

As Tyler drove, they discussed grades — of course, Tyler had got straight As as well — then Ryan's much better performance in Patents on Wednesday and Friday.

They arrived downtown, then to Kelsey's surprise, drove through it and over the West Seattle bridge.

"We're going to Alki," Kelsey said in delight. She loved Alki Beach, and they hadn't been since the summer.

"Can't keep a secret from Miss North," Tyler commented, and smiled at her.

After lunch at the great Mexican place Tyler had taken her the year before, they walked on the beach. It was cold, being April, but there were still a few hardy souls walking on the beach. Tyler held Kelsey's hand as the wind whipped her blonde ponytail.

"Warm enough?" Tyler asked.

"I'm fine," Kelsey replied.

It had been little more than a year ago when Kelsey had walked on this same beach with Tyler, discussing the possibility of his working for Bill Simon. Tyler had still been coming to grips with his new two-billion dollar trust, and he and Kelsey were slowly becoming friends.

Now as she held his warm hand and they walked along the quiet beach, Kelsey glanced at him and he smiled back at her. She leaned her head against his strong arm. A year later, there were no words that needed to be spoken, but a thousand things to say.

Over the next week, Kelsey began to feel like she was back into the rhythm of law school. As part of the Intellectual Property track, Kelsey, Ryan and Tyler were taking patent law as well as licensing, which Kelsey would be focusing on at Collins Nicol this upcoming summer. They would join Zach and Jessica in the follow up to their negotiation class — Complex Negotiation — which would teach them ways to prepare for high stakes, high value negotiations.

Again she began her mornings with a kiss from Tyler at the gym, then breakfast, followed by class. Tyler was immersed in Law Review, and it seemed to Kelsey that Jeffrey was on campus at least four times a week with Tactec business.

"I need to talk to Simon," Tyler said on Thursday after Jeffrey left, having delivered another file of paperwork to Tyler.

"You should just work for Tactec," Ryan said, delivering a spoonful of yogurt to Jessica's open mouth.

"Never," Tyler replied.

Tyler canceled his usual dates with Kelsey on Friday and Saturday, promising to make them up to her, but without telling her why. Kelsey spent Saturday making lemon tarts with Ryan and Jessica, and Sunday studying licensing.

Tyler and Brandon walked into the dining hall on Tuesday at lunch, holding trays. Kelsey smiled. She hadn't seen Tyler since Friday afternoon. He had sent messages to her every day, but she still had no idea why he had been gone.

"It's over," Brandon said to Ryan, sitting down at an empty space. He slid his tray onto the table.

"Tactec settled with Kinnon Martins," Tyler said, setting his tray next to Kelsey and sitting down. He gave her a kiss.

"No? Really? Congratulations," Ryan said to Brandon.

"Was this your project?" she asked.

Tyler nodded. "Bob asked me to drop by to remind my mother that Kinnon Martins was only getting in the way of integrating Chen Industries into Tactec," he said. "She didn't need the reminder, but she asked me to stick around her office until it was done. I'm sorry I couldn't tell you."

"They were still fighting at six this morning," Brandon said wearily.

"But it's over," Tyler said. "And what's our lesson?"

"Don't overbill Lisa Olsen," Brandon grinned.

"It's don't overbill your clients," Tyler corrected.

"I didn't get that," Brandon said.

"You're truly your father's son," Tyler said.

"I think we've clearly shown that my father didn't orchestrate the policy of overbilling for projects from Tactec," Brandon commented.

"Have you shown that?" Tyler asked.

Brandon shrugged. "I think he's paid enough, Mr. Olsen."

"Probably," Tyler said. Kelsey thought so too, knowing that the Kinnon family had been forced to file for bankruptcy.

"Tonight will be the first good night's sleep my father will have had in months," Brandon said, biting into his pizza. "Thanks for your help."

"There wasn't much for me to do. Lisa got bored once she found out that your dad wasn't behind the overbilling scheme."

"Who was?" Jessica asked. Brandon and Tyler looked at each other.

"Let's just say another partner saw an opportunity to pay for his alimony bills," Tyler said. "So what is your father going to do next?"

"I don't know. The bar complaint was dismissed, so maybe he'll reach out to a few people and try to get some consulting work," Brandon said.

Tyler nodded thoughtfully. "Did I miss anything?" he asked Kelsey.

"Ryan's lemon tarts. Otherwise, no," she replied.

"I missed you," he said to her.

"How sweet," Brandon said with sarcasm.

"Why are you here?" Jessica asked him.

"Because we need to find a girlfriend for Brandon," Ryan said, smiling at him.

"Please do," Brandon said.

"Who would date you?" Jessica asked. Brandon glared at her.

Tyler took a bite of his sandwich and chewed.

"Brandon," he said, as he finished, "why was your father against the trusts?"

"Yours and Ryan's?" Brandon asked.

"Yes," Tyler said.

"Like I said, because he figured you'd blow through them," Brandon said.

Tyler shook his head. "That's not why. You know as well as I do that we haven't seen any money yet, because that's the way the trust documents are written. So he knew we couldn't do that even if we wanted to. So why did he fight with Lisa?"

"I guess I don't know," Brandon said.

"Find out," Tyler replied, taking another bite of his sandwich.

On Saturday night, Kelsey opened the door of her apartment to Tyler and Ryan. Ryan was dressed up for a night on the town, while Tyler wore a navy cotton sweater and rolled-up khakis. Jessica walked out into the living room, wearing a beautiful black dress. It was quite a contrast to Kelsey's ripped jeans and pink Darrow Law t-shirt.

"Are you two seriously not going tonight?" Jessica asked, as Ryan took her hand.

"Seriously, we aren't," Kelsey replied. Tonight's student event was an all-campus dance, to be held at the dining hall. After three memorable dances with Tyler, Kelsey had refused to attend.

Ryan laughed. "We won't take photos," he said.

"We're not risking it," Tyler replied. He was just as in favor of missing the dance as Kelsey was.

"Darn. I thought we'd have some fun," Ryan said. Jessica smiled at him.

"Forget it," Kelsey said. "Go and have a good time," she said.

"Okay. Come on, Ryan, you're not going to convince them to embarrass themselves in public," Jessica said, pulling Ryan to the door.

"See you later," Kelsey said as they left.

"So do you want to dance?" Tyler said. Kelsey frowned at him.

"I was kidding," Tyler said. He put his arms around Kelsey, and kissed her.

"Three feet on the floor, Mr. Olsen," Kelsey said to him, referring to the rules at Tyler's summer boarding school. "There's a boy and a girl alone in a room."

"I thought your rule was 'don't get caught'?'" Tyler said, kissing her again.

"I was joking," Kelsey said.

"That's unfortunate," Tyler said.

"Stop teasing me. Tyler," Kelsey said. "Otherwise, I'm sending you home."

"If I can't tease you, what are we doing this evening?" Tyler asked her.

"You're helping me make muffins," Kelsey replied.

A few minutes later, Tyler's nose was dusted with flour.

"Stop eating my chocolate chips," Kelsey warned.

"There are plenty left," Tyler replied, eating another one.

Kelsey removed the gold-colored bag from his hands.

"I'm warning you," she said.

"Again? I'm getting into trouble a lot tonight. Maybe I will go home," Tyler said.

Kelsey looked up at him flirtatiously. "Really?" she cooed.

"Absolutely not," Tyler replied. "Stop looking at me like that," he said. Kelsey grinned. She poured the chocolate chips into a cup, and once it was full, handed the bag back to Tyler.

"Here. You can eat the rest," she said, pouring the cup of chocolate chips into the batter.

"I told you there were enough," Tyler said, removing a chocolate chip from the bag and eating it.

Kelsey ignored him and began stirring the batter.

"So I have a question for you."

"Okay," Kelsey said.

"When is Jasmine's wedding?" Tyler asked.

"Mid-July," Kelsey said.

"I was afraid of that. When?"

"I have to look at my phone," she replied. "Why?"

"The Tactec summer picnic," Tyler said.

Kelsey's face fell. "I totally forgot," she said, wiping her hands on her jeans. She walked over to the phone and pulled up her calendar.

"July 16th," she answered.

"Good," Tyler said. "Tactec is the 23rd."

"Great," Kelsey said.

"I need you to be there," Tyler said seriously.

Kelsey giggled. "You could ask Dara Smith."

"Not funny," Tyler said.

"What ever happened to her?"

"I don't know. I don't keep up with Ryan's models."

Kelsey picked up the spoon and stirred the batter for a final time.

"Do you want to put it into the pans?" Kelsey asked him.

Tyler shook his head.

"I don't need to learn to cook," he said.

"Of course you do."

"Nope. I plan on stealing Margaret from my mom after graduation," he said.

Kelsey giggled. "Well, I certainly can't complain about that plan," she said, picking up the prepared muffin pan, and portioning out the batter. "You're a good cook though. I loved your pasta at Valentines. It was so creative."

"Thanks. I did it for you."

"I know," Kelsey replied. "You're very sweet."

"Sweet on you," Tyler replied.

"Are you flirting with me again?" Kelsey asked.

"Finally. You noticed," Tyler said.

"I always notice. Because you're always doing it."

"I'd like to do something else," Tyler said. Kelsey looked at him. She wasn't about to dare to ask what he wanted to do. Tyler put his hand under her chin, and tipped her face up. He kissed her deeply.

His eyes sparkled, and Kelsey turned back to her batter.

"How am I expected to get through law school with you around?" Tyler asked her.

"I have the same problem," Kelsey said, taking the last of the batter out of the bowl, and putting into the muffin pan. She set the bowl aside and looked at him. Tyler was still looking at her.

Tyler stepped closer to her. He slid his hands down her bare arms, and took her hands. Then he kissed her again, more passionately than before. Kelsey felt a tingle up her spine. Tyler broke away from her.

"We should go out," Tyler said.

"What?" Kelsey said in surprise.

"Message me when you're ready," Tyler said, walking to the door.

"Where are you going?" Kelsey asked him.

"To take a cold shower," Tyler said testily. And he left.

Kelsey put the muffins into the hot oven, then went to her room to change. She changed into her new jeans and put on a different t-shirt and a blue cardigan. Once she had brushed her hair, the muffins were done. She turned off the oven, and put the muffins on the counter to cool. She picked up her phone and sent a message to Tyler, who asked her to come over to his apartment. Kelsey put the phone in her pocket, placed her wallet and keys in a purse that she tossed over her shoulder, and left. She knocked on Tyler's door. And he opened it.

To Kelsey's surprise, Tyler's hair was wet. He was drying it with a towel. He was wearing jeans and a forest green sweater.

"You really took a shower?" Kelsey asked him, disbelievingly.

"I said I was going to," Tyler said petulantly. He left her in the living room and walked into the bathroom. He returned a second later, without the towel.

"Why are you smiling like that?" Tyler demanded.

"No reason," Kelsey said in amusement.

Tyler surveyed her. "There should be a law for people like you," he commented.

"Like what?"

"Being so alluring should be a crime," Tyler said, leaning over and kissing her. He looked at her and took her hand. "We're leaving now," he said sharply.

"Where are we going?" Kelsey asked.

"Out," Tyler replied. Kelsey giggled as he pulled her out of the door.

To Kelsey's delight, Tyler took her to an ice cream shop on Capitol Hill. To her interest, it was across the street from Cal Anderson Park, where they had once had a very passionate kiss, and had a major turning point in their relationship. Tyler glanced at her as they walked hand-in-hand into the ice cream shop.

"Let's make some new, happier memories here," he said to her.

Kelsey nodded. They looked up at the board of flavors.

"What do you want?"

"Mint. Although the salted caramel looks tempting," Kelsey replied.

"Get both," Tyler said.

Kelsey shook her head no. "They won't taste good together."

"Get mint and chocolate then," Tyler said.

"Why?"

"I'll get salted caramel. We can share," Tyler said.

They ordered cones. Mint with chocolate on top for Kelsey, salted caramel with chocolate on the bottom for Tyler. They switched cones and walked over to the park.

"You aren't wearing heels tonight," Tyler commented, taking a lick of the chocolate.

"You aren't driving Ryan's Porsche," Kelsey said. She took a bite of the caramel ice cream. It was perfect.

"I should have taken it tonight. He's on campus anyway," Tyler commented.

"I'm not dressed for it," Kelsey said. "Can I eat all of this?" she asked him.

"Yes. I really just wanted chocolate," Tyler replied. They strolled up the gentle slope. It was a pleasant evening, so there were a lot of people out. Kids playing on the playground, teens sitting on the grass. Tyler and Kelsey found a ledge near the playground and sat down to enjoy their ice cream.

After a few minutes, they switched cones. Kelsey's mint was as delectable as the caramel, and thanks to the palate-clearing chocolate in between, she managed to enjoy all of the flavors.

"So what's with you?" Kelsey asked Tyler.

He smiled and took a lick of ice cream. "I really enjoyed my vacation with you," he said simply.

"Me too. So?" Kelsey said.

"I don't know, Kels," Tyler said. "I guess I just started thinking about our future," he said.

"Hmm," she said.

"There's that hmm again. Don't you think about our future?" Tyler asked her.

"Nope," Kelsey said, taking a bite of ice cream.

"You're kidding," Tyler said.

"It's true. As soon as I think about marrying you, I put it out of my mind. Not that I don't want to," Kelsey quickly added, seeing the pained look on Tyler's face. "But any future together is too far off," she said.

"Why?"

"We don't graduate for another year. The bar exam is after that. I can't think that far away."

"You could," Tyler pointed out.

"I don't want to," Kelsey replied. "There's too many things that could happen between now and then."

"Like what?" Tyler asked her.

"You could fall out of love with me," Kelsey said.

"Impossible. You are my world," Tyler replied.

"Feelings change, Tyler."

"Not mine," He took a bite of the chocolate ice cream in his cone. "Maybe yours?" he mused.

"I don't think so," Kelsey said. She sighed. "I don't know, Tyler. It just seems too early."

Tyler sighed and thought for a moment. "I don't mean to push you," he finally said. "I think that since every other part of my life seems to be planned out for me, it would be nice to have a part to look forward to."

"I'm honored," Kelsey said. "I do love you, Tyler."

Tyler nodded and took a bite of his cone. He sat silently for a moment. "I love you too," he finally replied.

After they finished their cones in silence, they walked through the park hand-in-hand. Kelsey glanced at Tyler, who seemed to be thinking. She was thinking a lot too. Kelsey believed every word that she had said to Tyler, but in her heart, she knew there was something more, another reason that she didn't feel as secure with Tyler as he did with her.

Kelsey didn't want to admit it, but she had never forgotten Dylan's prediction that Tyler wouldn't be hers. She had been reminded of it when she had seen him in Portland, and it had been lodged in her mind ever since. No matter how confident Tyler was that his future was with her, there was always an annoying feeling that things could go wrong, and that they could go wrong fast.

So her armor was up. And she felt terrible, because Tyler had fought through his own defenses — which had been considerable — and given his heart to her.

"Do you want to go to the bookstore?" Tyler asked her. Kelsey looked at him, startled. "Are you okay?" Tyler asked her in concern.

"Just thinking," Kelsey replied. She gave him a smile. "Sure. Let's go."

A few minutes later, they climbed up the stairs to one of Seattle's most beloved bookstores. Tyler held the door open for Kelsey and they walked in.

"It feels small compared to Powell's," Tyler commented.

"There's no comparison," Kelsey said. "But I like it here."

"Where do you want to look?" he asked.

"Magazines," Kelsey said.

"I'll be up in languages," Tyler said.

"Is your Norwegian still lacking, Mr. Olsen?" Kelsey teased.

"Margaret dropped by to deliver lunch and say hi when I was with my mother. She used the word *uvitende* to describe me three times in our conversation."

"Stupid?" Kelsey guessed.

"Good guess, you're close. It means ignorant. She's going to cut off my gossip if I don't get it together. It's my top priority."

"Okay," Kelsey giggled.

"No really. Jeffrey won't gossip about my mother, and Martin doesn't pay any attention to what's happening in Medina. Margaret's critical."

"Why?"

"I need to know what Lisa's planning next. Bob really has me worried," Bob had told Tyler that Jeffrey and Lisa were plotting something, and Bob had guessed it had something to do with Tyler.

"Better get to work then," Kelsey grinned.

Tyler kissed her on the forehead. "See you in a minute," he replied. Tyler walked off, heading for the stairs.

Kelsey wandered over to the magazines. Jasmine had asked her to think about the style of her bridesmaid gown. The color, bright pink, had already been decided, but Jasmine had said she was open to the style. So Kelsey wanted to find anything that would detract from the hideousness of the color.

Kelsey browsed through the selection of bridal magazines. They were huge, and crammed full of advertisements for dresses. She narrowed her choices down to three, and carrying them in her hands, walked upstairs to join Tyler.

She found him leaning over a table, reading an intermediate Norwegian language book.

"Find anything?" she asked. Tyler looked up. He glanced at the magazines she was holding.

"Is there something you're trying to tell me?" he asked with a smile. Kelsey looked at where he was looking, and frowned.

"Jazz is getting married, remember?" she replied.

"Right. I had forgotten," Tyler said, closing the book and standing.

"Are you getting that?" Kelsey asked.

"No," Tyler said, returning the book to the shelf. "My Norwegian is better than that. Maybe I'll hire a tutor."

"A tutor to understand your chef," Kelsey said.

"A tutor to understand my informer," Tyler corrected. "It would be worth every penny."

They returned to the first floor, where Tyler purchased the bridal magazines for Kelsey.

"I can't wait to see the bright pink dresses. I'm on team Jasmine," Tyler commented. Kelsey stuck her tongue out at him, and he laughed.

They left the bookstore holding hands, with Tyler carrying the heavy magazines in a paper bag in his other hand.

"I guess I'm wondering if you won't think about our future because it took me so long to ask you out," Tyler mused as they headed back to his car.

"Like I'm punishing you?" Kelsey asked.

"Maybe. I don't think you're doing it on purpose. But I just wonder," Tyler said.

Kelsey thought for a moment, then she said,

"You know, I've kind of been beating myself up over the same thing. Why won't I think about our future together? But I just realized something."

"Yes?" Tyler asked curiously.

"You haven't actually asked me to share my future with you. I haven't heard a marriage proposal. For all I know, this is how we will always be. Going out, spending time together. I'm committed to that, and for now, so are you. But you haven't committed to anything else, so maybe I don't need to think about it at all."

Tyler scowled. "This is the problem with dating a law student."

"What?"

"They can always figure out the loopholes," Tyler said. He pulled Kelsey's hand up to his lips and kissed it gently.

"Fine," he said. "You're off the hook until I ask you to marry me."

Kelsey smiled, finally at peace with her heart. With Tyler's track record, that question could be years away.

The next day, Jessica and Kelsey were sitting in their living room, thumbing through the bridal magazines as they waited for Tyler and Ryan to come over. The boys were taking them to brunch in the Greenlake neighborhood of Seattle.

"How about this one?" Jessica asked, pointing at a fuchsia dress.

"It's worse seeing them than imagining them," Kelsey commented. There was a knock on the door and Kelsey stood up. "I'm going to cry soon," she said as she walked over to the door.

"Hi," Ryan said, greeting Kelsey. He walked in, as did Tyler, who gave her a kiss. Ryan walked over to the sofa and sat next to Jessica. "What are you reading?" he asked her.

"Kelsey's bridal magazines," Jessica said.

Ryan looked at Kelsey over the sofa. "Are you getting married, Miss North?"

"No time soon, Mr. Perkins," Kelsey replied.

"That's what you think," Ryan said. He snuggled next to Jessica. "Have you seen anything you like?" he asked her.

"Actually, I did," Jessica said putting the magazine that she was holding down and picking up another one up from the coffee table. "I saw this beautiful black-and-white wedding in this one." Jessica began flipping through the pages, then stopped abruptly. "Why are you asking me?" she demanded.

"No reason," Ryan said innocently. Jessica pondered him for a moment, then resumed flipping pages.

"This one," she said, stopping on a page and handing the magazine to him.

"Pretty," Ryan said, looking at it in interest.

Tyler glanced over Jessica's shoulder. "Well, if you get your birthday wish…" he began.

"He won't," Jessica snapped.

"Hope springs eternal," Tyler commented as Ryan flipped through the pages, then turned the magazine over to see the cover. Tyler turned to Kelsey, and slipped his arms around her waist. He kissed her gently.

"Hi," Kelsey said.

"Hello, Miss North," Tyler said, giving her a hug.

A half hour later, Kelsey and Tyler met Ryan and Jessica at a restaurant across the street from Green Lake in northern Seattle. They had left the apartment and driven up separately.

"I wish it wasn't too cold to sit outside," Kelsey commented as Tyler helped her into her seat. "It's beautiful up here."

"Isn't it? Wow," Jessica said.

"You haven't been here before?" Tyler asked Kelsey. She shook her head.

"You haven't been anywhere in Seattle," Ryan commented to Kelsey. "It's not like Port Townsend is far away."

"We only came to Seattle to go Christmas shopping," Kelsey said. "We have a store to run."

"I guess. Didn't you come over with your girlfriends?" Ryan said.

"Rarely. And I wouldn't have come up here," Kelsey replied.

"I suppose you wouldn't," Ryan said, turning back to his menu.

"You can learn all about Seattle now that you live here," Tyler said to her. "What are you having for brunch?"

"French toast, maybe," Kelsey said.

"It won't be as good as mine," Ryan commented.

"Of course not. But you aren't cooking brunch today, so I'll have to make do," Kelsey replied.

"Are you really going to cook every day this summer?" Jessica asked.

"If you live with us I will," Ryan said.

"So make sure you live with us," Tyler commented. "Both of you."

"We'll see," Jessica said.

"Portland was fun with all four of us," Ryan said.

"It was," Jessica agreed.

"Wouldn't you like to have that experience every day?" Ryan asked.

Jessica looked at him. "I said, we'll see, Ryan," she said.

Ryan pouted and Jessica giggled and gave him a kiss.

"You're so impatient," she said, turning back to her menu.

"I just want us to be together," Ryan replied.

They ordered their meals and their drinks arrived. Kelsey and Jessica had ordered hot chocolate, and Jessica spooned some of her whipped cream into Ryan's mouth. He surveyed Jessica with his bright blue eyes.

Tyler smiled at the two of them.

"Are you looking forward to next weekend, Jess?" Tyler asked.

Jessica nodded. "I am," she replied.

Ryan and Jessica would be joining Lisa Olsen at a yoga retreat at her Medina house the following Sunday. Several Tactec executives would participate as well, including Ryan's boss from the Legal Department. Ryan had helped plan it with Lisa, but Tyler had declined to go on both his and Kelsey's behalf.

"Lisa's bringing in a top teacher from San Diego, Sangeeta Sahni. It should be really good," Ryan commented.

"Is Margaret cooking?" Tyler asked.

Ryan shook his head. "Thrive is catering it," he said.

"Raw food?" Kelsey asked.

"No. Just vegan," Ryan replied.

"What does Mom think of that?" Tyler asked. Lisa Olsen didn't think highly of vegetarians.

"It's just one meal," Ryan commented. "She can go back to her paleo diet at dinner."

"You're really taking yoga seriously," Kelsey said to them.

"Jess wants to teach next year," Ryan said proudly.

"You should try it, Kels," Jessica said.

"No, thank you," Kelsey replied as their food arrived.

Everyone received their meals. Kelsey dug into her Belgian waffle, which she had got after discovering that the French toast was made with cognac batter. Although she wasn't adverse to the occasional splash of wine cooked in a sauce, she didn't want anything that would awaken her long-dormant addiction.

"Did you hear from Simon?" Kelsey asked Tyler between bites. He had mentioned on the ride home from their date last night that he had left Simon a message about rearranging his schedule in light of all of the Tactec obligations he was expecting to have this summer.

"This morning. He said I can work all day on Saturday."

"All day?" Kelsey said in concern. A day at Simon and Associates began at 8 a.m. and could last past midnight.

"Until five," Tyler clarified.

"That's better." Tyler had worked what Simon considered half-days on Saturday last summer, working from 9 to 1 or 2 in the afternoon. Of course, there had been more than a few Saturdays when the half day lasted until 6. Perhaps midnight was a better estimate.

"No wonder you want Kelsey to live with you. You won't see her otherwise," Jessica commented, biting into her toast.

"I'll go over to Tyler's office," Kelsey said.

"And do my work for me," Tyler grinned.

"Exactly," Kelsey giggled.

"How many interns will he have this summer?" Ryan asked.

"He's hired a total of five," Tyler said.

"How many will last past July 4th?" Ryan teased.

"One," Tyler said. "Me."

"I really can't believe you're doing this again," Ryan said.

"It's the last time. I'll be in Lisa's clutches next summer," Tyler replied.

"What does she want with you this year?" Ryan asked.

"Some big project. She wants me to work for her two days a week during August."

"So you'll be in her clutches this summer," Jessica commented.

"I'm trying not to think about that, Jess," Tyler said.

"So you'll work for both Simon and Tactec in August?" Kelsey asked.

Tyler nodded.

"What's your title?" Jessica asked.

"Lisa's little boy," Ryan teased.

"Funny. Actually, highly-paid consultant to the CEO."

"Lisa's paying you?" Ryan asked.

"A lot," Tyler said. "She said that I'll be representing her, and she wants me to take it seriously."

"You take everything seriously," Ryan commented.

"I'll take the money anyway," Tyler said.

They finished brunch, Tyler paid the bill, and they left the restaurant.

They crossed the street and walked over to the Green Lake path. Green Lake was a popular destination for bikers, walkers, and joggers no matter the weather, and although it was a cold day, the sun was shining. The group joined the walkers on the pedestrian side of the path encircling the lake.

Ryan put his arm around Jessica's shoulders, while Tyler and Kelsey followed behind, holding hands. Tyler was wearing Kelsey's Christmas scarf.

"I guess I'd better keep a change of clothes at Simon's," Tyler said to her.

"Are you sure that you can manage all of this? Simon and your Mom?"

"Tactec is paying me by the hour, so they won't waste my time."

"But you don't know what you'll be doing yet?"

"Not yet. Mom said I'd enjoy it, whatever it is. I guess I'll find out more this summer."

"At least Tactec is downtown. Or will you have to go to Bellevue?"

"Just downtown. I need to be close so I can work at Simon's after I'm done at Tactec."

"I'm always going to be in your office, aren't I?" Kelsey teased.

"There's no reason not to enjoy your summer. You should hang out with Jess and Ryan."

"I'd rather be with you," Kelsey said. Tyler squeezed her hand.

A small pack of runners passed them. Jessica's curly ponytail bobbed as they walked next to the shore of the lake. They passed a few senior citizens who were fishing.

"What's that island?" Jessica asked, pointing out into the lake.

"Duck Island," Ryan said.

"Is anything there?" Jessica asked.

"It's off-limits," Ryan said.

"Ha," Tyler commented.

"Something you want to tell the class, Mr. Olsen?" Jessica asked, looking back.

"Ryan should stop pretending that he's innocent," Tyler said.

"You went with me," Ryan pouted.

"I'll admit it," Tyler replied.

"You have less to hide," Jessica said.

"That's certainly true," Tyler replied.

"Fine. Tyler and I went there in high school with a bunch of our classmates. I admitted it, okay?"

"Was that hard?" Tyler said.

"Why did you go?" Jessica asked.

"Why do you think?" Tyler asked Jessica sarcastically.

"I have no idea," Jessica said honestly.

"Shush. My Jessica is actually innocent," Ryan said.

"They went to party, Jess," Kelsey said.

"'Party' is Kelsey's euphemism for 'drink,'" Tyler said. He glanced at

Kelsey. "You're as bad as Ryan. What do you have to hide?" he said.

"Obviously more than you," Kelsey said. Tyler laughed.

They looped around the south edge of the lake and passed by the boathouse. A stream of bicyclists, skaters and runners passed by them.

"Look!" Jessica said excitedly, pointing. "Look," she repeated, lowering her voice. Kelsey's eyes followed where Jessica was pointing. A mama duck was leading four baby ducklings into the water.

"So cute!" Kelsey said beaming. They stopped with several other duck watchers as the last of the ducklings trundled into the water. Ryan held Jessica around the waist as the ducks swam away. Ryan kissed Jessica. She glared at him.

"Forget it. I'm not having five kids," she said.

"The duck had four," Ryan said.

"I'm not a duck," Jessica said

"We're Catholic. We're supposed to have all the children we can," Ryan said.

"You aren't Catholic," Jessica said dismissively.

"Bob is. Close enough," Ryan replied.

"I'm not marrying you," Jessica said.

"Of course you are. And we're going to have lots of babies," Ryan replied petulantly.

"Do you have to put up with this?" Jessica asked Kelsey.

Kelsey grinned and shook her head.

"I'm Lutheran," Tyler offered.

"A heathen," Jessica teased.

"*Extra Ecclesiam nulla salus,*" Tyler replied. Jessica giggled.

"Finally some Latin I understand," she commented.

"I don't," Ryan said, looking at both of them.

"You would if you were really Catholic, and not just pretending. 'Outside the Church there is no salvation,'" Tyler translated.

"So we're doomed," Kelsey said.

"Afraid so. Sorry," Jessica replied.

"How can you be Catholic and not want lots of kids?" Ryan asked her.

"Two is lots," Jessica replied. "Why are we discussing this?"

"I want five," Ryan pouted.

"Like I said, I'm not marrying you, so it doesn't matter," Jessica said.

"That's what you think," Ryan replied haughtily. Jessica giggled.

They resumed their walk around the lake. Tyler held Kelsey's hand as Jessica continued looking out for more ducklings.

"We should come here and run sometime," Tyler said to Kelsey.

"Maybe. I'm enjoying the walk. It's really beautiful here."

"It's like the lagoon in Port Townsend," Tyler commented.

"You're right. I hadn't thought about that," Kelsey said.

"Do you like the neighborhood?" Ryan asked Jessica.

She looked over at the houses that surrounded the lake.

"It's nice. Imagine waking up to a view of the lake."

"The neighborhood is really family-friendly," Ryan said helpfully.

"Is it?" Jessica asked, amused.

"Yes. It is," Ryan pouted.

"Perfect for large families?" Jessica teased.

"Perfect," Ryan replied.

"Then I don't need to live up here," Jessica said.

"You do too. I don't know why you're teasing me so much today," Ryan said grumpily.

"I just don't want to think about getting married or having kids today. I have a tax class to figure out," Jessica said. "We can talk about marriage this summer."

"We can?" Ryan asked brightly.

"Talk about. Not get married," Jessica clarified.

"Oh," Ryan said in disappointment.

"You're like Bob," Jessica said.

"No, I'm not. If I was, we would already be married," Ryan said.

"You asked me last summer. Of course then you were joking," Jessica said.

"I wasn't," Ryan said seriously.

"There was no ring," Jessica said.

"Do you require one?" Ryan asked in surprise.

"Of course. A big, fat diamond," Jessica teased.

"Okay," Ryan said.

"Jess is like your mom, Kels," Tyler commented.

Kelsey giggled.

"What do you mean?" Ryan asked.

"Kelsey's mom wouldn't say yes without a ring," Tyler said. "I heard the story at Thanksgiving."

"So we'll go ring shopping," Ryan said happily.

"No, we won't. Ryan, stop nagging me. I still have a year and a semester of law school. We can plan on marriage after we take the bar," Jessica said.

"That's a year and a half away. I'm not waiting that long," Ryan commented.

"Then you should find someone else to marry," Jessica said.

Ryan glared at her. "I'm marrying you," he said. "This year. I said so."

"That's what you think," Jessica retorted.

"That's what I know," Ryan said petulantly.

"It's like you two are on the playground," Tyler commented.

"I don't understand why Jess is so difficult," Ryan said. "I know you want to marry me," he said to her. "You're playing hard to get again."

"I am hard to get," Jessica replied.

"Now that I've got you, I'm going to keep you," Ryan said, hugging her shoulders.

They completed their walk around the lake, and headed back to their respective cars. Ryan and Jess headed to the restaurant that would be catering next weekend's yoga retreat, to finalize the menu, while Tyler and Kelsey headed to Whole Foods to take cupcakes back home. Tyler took two packages of cupcakes off the shelf.

"They are really cute," Kelsey said, as they walked over to the fruit aisle.

"Ryan's determined. I have to give him credit," Tyler said. "Jess threatening to leave has been a real wake-up call for him."

"He seems nervous, and that's strange for Ryan," Kelsey agreed. "Does he really want to marry her this year?"

"I think he's quite serious," Tyler said.

"He doesn't want to wait until after graduation?" Kelsey asked.

"Ryan's not exactly known for his patience. What do you think Jess will say if he asks her?"

Kelsey thought for a moment.

"Before Jess decided to stay here, I would have have said, she definitely would say no. But now that she's picked Ryan over her family, I'd say it's 50/50."

"What do you mean picked Ryan over her family?" Tyler asked curiously. Kelsey didn't want to break any confidences, so she chose her words carefully.

"Let's just say that Jessica's father isn't too happy that she's planning on staying at Darrow."

"That's crazy. It's the best law school in the country and he wants her to come home?" Tyler said. "I don't get that."

"Jess doesn't have a lot of freedom, when it comes to him," Kelsey said.

"It must have been a really big decision for her to refuse her father then," Tyler mused.

"The biggest," Kelsey agreed.

After her memorable weekend with Tyler, it was time for Kelsey to get back to work. She had settled back into the new semester, but there were a few things she needed to attend to.

Tuesday afternoon, Kelsey gathered her birth certificate, checkbook, driver's license, and a completed form, and headed downtown to apply for her passport. After a quick stop for her photo and to make a copy of her ID, she walked into the passport office. A half hour — and one hundred and thirty five dollars — later, she was on her way to being able to travel the world.

Jessica and Kelsey were sitting in the boys' apartment as Tyler and Zach were explaining various methods for valuing intellectual property on Sunday afternoon. Ryan sat happily cuddled up to Jessica, listening as well. Jessica, who wasn't taking licensing, was reading her tax casebook, gearing up for her third semester of her most dreaded class.

"So there are three ways to value IP. Cost, which means that we look at the actual costs for getting or creating the IP. In calculating the costs we would combine the direct costs, like the salary for the programmer, the indirect costs, overhead and profit for the IP," Zachary said. He paused as Kelsey typed into her iPad.

"Second, we can value IP by looking at the market. What are people paying for this kind of IP right now? The problem with valuing IP with the market, is that a lot of the time the technology is so new and so different, there isn't a good way to determine what the market cost really would be," Zach continued.

"Third, and most commonly used, is valuing IP by the expected income. I imagine, although Mr. Olsen won't tell me, that this is the way that Tactec determined that the extraordinary price that they paid for Chen Industries was worth it," Zach glared at Tyler, who grinned.

"Notice that I'm not worried that the SEC is going to knock on my door for giving insider information to you," Tyler commented.

"Aren't you going to get three completely different values from these three methods?" Kelsey asked.

"Sure, but they might all be right. Like beauty, the value of IP is in the eye of the beholder. The IP that Chen Industries holds is worth a lot more to Tactec than it was to Chen, simply because Tactec has the means to license it out to other companies. There no one way to value IP, so you have to decide how you're going to approach any purchase," Tyler said.

"It's less relevant to you, because as a lawyer, your client will probably already have done a lot of the valuation for themselves and will know what a fair price will be. But it's helpful to be able to understand the methodology that they have used," Zach said.

"As a lawyer?" Jessica interjected.

"Jess, remember, I'll be working for a venture capital firm. We do valuations for a living, otherwise we'll pay too much to invest in IP companies," Zach said.

"Right, of course," Jessica said. She returned to her book.

"Good question," Ryan said, snuggling up against her.

"Are you even paying attention?" Tyler asked him.

"Nope," Ryan replied. "I'm going to work for Legal. Lisa just tells us what to do."

"And soon Tyler will be telling Legal what to do," Zach said.

"Ha," Tyler said, frowning. "Let's hope not."

"Let's take a break," Zach said, sitting down in one of the chairs. "So how's Lisa's board?" he asked Tyler.

"Don't ask. I swear, I wonder why she even has a board. She could just buy a rubber stamp, because that's all that they do," Tyler commented.

"She's required to have a board," Zach pointed out.

"A potted plant would give her more opposition," Tyler said.

"What are you so grumpy about the board for?" Zach said.

"My stock has dropped. I'm not happy about that," Tyler said.

"Yeah, because you now have 1.99 billion instead of two?" Zach commented. "Cry me a river."

Tyler smiled. "I know it doesn't matter to you, but the stock should be going up, not down."

"Maybe you should start a proxy fight. Wrest control of the board away from Lisa," Zach teased.

"Funny," Tyler said.

"So what are you going to do about it?" Zach asked.

"Complain. Of course, Lisa's not listening," Tyler said.

"She never does," Zach commented.

"That's true," Tyler replied.

"At least you only have to work for her part-time this summer. I don't know how I'm going to deal with my parents again. At least I don't have to live with them."

"Where are you living, Zach?" Kelsey asked him.

"I got my own place for the summer. Nice and far away from Medina."

"Far? It's in Bellevue," Tyler said. "You could walk there from your parents' house."

"Do not underestimate the benefits of coming home, eating dinner, and not having to discuss all of your screw-ups in the office. It will be heaven," Zachary replied.

"You've got a point," Tyler said.

"Of course I do. I bet Lisa won't criticize every mistake you make this summer," Zach said.

"True, it isn't her management style," Tyler said.

"What is?" Jessica asked.

"Firing the one who made the mistake," Tyler replied.

"But she'll never fire you," Zach said.

"I know. She'll be like Simon," Tyler said.

"I couldn't believe he never fired you. I completely expected you to have most of the summer off," Ryan commented.

"He needs someone around to torture," Tyler commented drolly.

"Like Lisa," Zach said.

"Like your mom," Tyler retorted.

"Don't remind me," Zach said. "My parents are a nightmare, but I'm focusing on the positive. Evenings and weekends in my own place."

"So what will working for Bob be like?" Kelsey asked.

"Easy," Tyler said.

"Fun," Ryan commented.

"Really?" Jess said.

"Bob won't make you do anything," Zach said. "Everyone loves working for Bob."

"How does anything get done then?" Kelsey asked.

"When Bob needs to yell at someone, he sends them to Lisa," Tyler said. "The threat of dealing with Ms. Olsen keeps everyone in line."

Jessica laughed. "Tyler, you have an interesting viewpoint about your mother."

"What do you mean?"

"She's your mom, but she's also your CEO. How do you separate them out?"

"I don't," Tyler said. "I only know her as Lisa Olsen, CEO. And Mom. There's no divide in my head. She and Bob started the company when I was too small. I've never known her as anything else."

"No lullabies?" Jessica asked.

"I think she read annual reports to get me to sleep," Tyler replied.

"That would knock anyone out," Zach laughed.

"What about you, Ryan?" Kelsey asked him.

"What about me?" Ryan asked.

"What do you think about Bob?"

"Bob's cool," Ryan shrugged.

"Comparing Lisa and Bob is like comparing apples and oranges. They aren't even opposites, it's like they are on different planets," Zach interjected.

"True," Tyler agreed.

"How do they work together then?" Jessica asked.

"It's like Bob said when we were camping. He lets Lisa do everything she wants. He does the rest. And everyone's happy," Tyler replied.

"Especially Bob," Zach commented.

"He's certainly gotten very rich with his method," Jessica said.

"Speaking of, where's the new plane, Ryan?" Zach asked.

"He'll take delivery in August," Ryan replied.

"What's he buying? 737?" Zach asked.

"Gulfstream. Bob's too cheap to buy a 737," Ryan said.

"Cheap? He's buying a second plane," Jessica said.

"It only holds 16 people," Ryan commented.

"Only," Kelsey said, rolling her eyes. Jessica giggled.

"You are so spoiled," Zach said. "Do you know how many planes my parents own? Zero. We always fly coach."

"We used to," Jessica whispered to Kelsey.

"I just think he should have gotten a bigger plane," Ryan shrugged.

"To hold the baseball team worth of kids you want to have?" Jessica asked.

Ryan grinned at her. "Exactly. Are you ready?"

"Ready for what?"

"To marry me and start having babies."

"As if," Jessica said.

"I can't believe you're thinking about getting married," Zach said to Ryan. "Kim's right. You have changed."

"I've met the most perfect woman in the world. I'm not letting her out of my sight," Ryan said, leaning his head on Jessica's shoulder.

"Do you guys want to go to Norwegian Independence Day?" Ryan asked at lunch on Wednesday.

"I didn't know Norway wasn't always independent," Jessica said.

"It wasn't," Tyler commented. "It's really called Constitution Day, though."

"Why should we go? What's happening?" Jessica asked.

"There's a parade, and this year, Lisa's in it," Ryan said.

"Your mom?" Jessica asked in surprise.

"Every few years my grandmother and Margaret gang up on my mother to accept the invitation to be the Grand Marshal. This is one of those years," Tyler said.

"Why do they have to gang up on her?" Kelsey asked.

"It's a day away from work," Tyler said. "There's a long luncheon, plus the parade itself. Ryan and I are just planning going to the parade that evening. It's on a Tuesday this year."

"It's not on the weekend?" Jessica asked.

"It's always on May 17th," Tyler replied.

"Is Margaret going?"

"Of course, it's her day off," Tyler said. "She never misses being in Ballard on Syttende Mai."

"Soot-in..." Jessica tried to repeat the phrase, but failed.

"Syttende Mai. May 17th," Tyler said.

"Oh," Jessica said. "Sure, I'll go."

"Me, too," Kelsey said. "It sounds like fun."

"It is. I haven't been in years though," Tyler said.

"We used to go with Margaret," Ryan offered.

"Wear red, white and blue," Tyler said.

It was Saturday night, the Saturday before the Friday that the Law Review would go to the publisher. This time last year, Tyler had been a virtual prisoner, toiling away in the Law Review offices. But today, he took Kelsey's hand, and they were heading to a sushi restaurant in the Fremont neighborhood.

"I'm really surprised to see you," Kelsey said to Tyler.

"I'm surprised to be here," Tyler replied.

"Christian's girlfriend is awesome," Kelsey said.

The Law Review Editor's girlfriend had stolen Christian's keys to the Law Review office and locked it, so everyone could have a final night off. Christian, who had a good sense of humor, and also enjoyed having a life outside of Law Review, had accepted defeat and told everyone to report tomorrow. Tyler had messaged Kelsey instantly.

"Remember this for next year. You can be awesome too," Tyler said to her.

"I can only meddle so much. You are responsible for putting out two Law Review issues," Kelsey said.

"Just remind me that I have a life. With you," Tyler said, kissing her. She smiled at him, and he opened the door of the restaurant. They walked in, and Tyler said to the server, "Two, please." The server nodded and walked them over to two seats next to each other. They sat down, and Kelsey looked around.

Tyler had brought her to a kaiten sushi restaurant, where the sushi passed by them on a conveyor belt. A seemingly never-ending variety of sushi passed by their eyes.

"Are you hungry?" Tyler asked her.

"Yes. It's good you're a billionaire," Kelsey said quietly.

Tyler laughed. "It's not that expensive. Eat what you want."

"Is this my payment for the next Tactec picnic?" Kelsey asked him.

"If it is, I'm getting off cheap," Tyler replied. He picked a plate of sushi off of the belt and placed it between them. Kelsey picked up a pair of black plastic chopsticks with glee. She loved sushi.

Tyler picked up his own chopsticks as Kelsey took a piece of the salmon sushi and placed it into her mouth.

"You're quite skilled with chopsticks, Miss North," Tyler said with amusement.

"Gotta eat," Kelsey replied, taking another piece and clearing the plate. Tyler took another plate of salmon sushi off the conveyor belt.

"This one's mine," Tyler teased.

"That's what you think," Kelsey said.

"We aren't even married yet, and you're treating everything like community property," Tyler said.

"We're in a common-law marriage," Kelsey said. "That's what you said when you were eating my ice cream."

"I was hoping you had forgotten that," Tyler replied.

"That you said we were married, or that you ate my ice cream?" Kelsey asked.

"The ice cream, of course. I'd love to be married to you."

"You say that now. I'm going to be a nightmare," Kelsey said.

Tyler shook his head. "You're the woman of my dreams." He picked up a piece of sushi and ate it. Kelsey took a plate of sushi rolls off of the conveyor belt. Tyler reached over and picked one up. He popped it into his mouth.

"Hey!" Kelsey said.

"Mmm. Avocado. I'll have another," Tyler said, reaching over with his own chopsticks. He took another sushi roll.

"Get your own."

"This is mine. Everything you have is mine," Tyler replied.

"You wish," Kelsey said.

"I certainly do," Tyler said, without looking at her.

"Are you flirting with me again?" Kelsey demanded.

"Of course. Why do you think I take you out?" Tyler said.

"To get away from Law Review," Kelsey replied.

Tyler laughed. "Well, there is that," he agreed.

Kelsey took another plate off the conveyor belt, leaving the avocado rolls to Tyler, who had eaten half of them.

"Did you want something to drink?" a server asked them.

"Water for me. Kels?"

"Make it two," she replied. The server walked off, and Kelsey looked at the plate of sushi she had taken off the belt.

"What is that?" Tyler asked curiously.

"I don't know, but it looked good," She poked at it with a chopstick. "I think there's crab."

As quick as lightning, Tyler took one of the rice rolls and ate it.

"It is crab. It's delicious," he said, smiling at her.

Kelsey burst into delighted laughter. "You're really annoying me," she said.

"You have to learn to eat faster," Tyler said.

"I'm an only child. I don't have siblings to compete against."

"Neither do I," Tyler replied.

"You have Ryan."

"Ryan's no competition," Tyler said definitively.

"You are so arrogant," Kelsey said, eating a rice roll.

"Thank you," Tyler said brightly.

"It wasn't meant as a complement," Kelsey said.

"However, I took it as one," Tyler said, placing his chopsticks to the side of an empty plate and looking at the offerings traveling by their eyes. He took one of the plates and set it between them.

"Shrimp tempura," he said, taking a bite.

"Yum," Kelsey said, taking one for herself. She had finished the crab rolls, and there was a small stack of empty plates growing between her and Tyler. Tyler took a bottle of soy sauce and poured a small amount of it next to the tempura rolls. Kelsey looked at the conveyor belt.

"Was that a cupcake?" she asked as something that looked like one passed by.

"Dessert," Tyler confirmed.

"They've thought of everything," Kelsey said. Tyler took his now-empty plate and placed it on the stack in front of them.

"Yes, they have. What am I going to eat now?" Tyler looked over at the table space in front of Kelsey expectantly. "Why don't you have something?"

"I'm waiting for you to pick something first," Kelsey replied.

"Is this a race?"

"I just know that whatever I pick, you're going to eat."

"Not necessarily," Tyler said. "I won't eat that." he said, as several plates trundled by.

"What won't you eat?" Kelsey asked. She had missed what he pointed to.

"You'll have to figure it out," he replied, deftly removing a plate from the belt.

"What's that? It looks like fried chicken," Kelsey said. She picked up her chopsticks and took one of the battered pieces.

"It's fried chicken," Tyler said as she chewed it.

"Is that Japanese?"

"It's called *karaage* there, but yes, it's Japanese."

"I guess everyone likes fried meat," Kelsey said, taking another.

"Particularly a Seattleite named Kelsey North."

"I'm from Port Townsend," she replied, swallowing.

"Not any more. The people of Port Townsend are sweet and friendly. You're a hard-boiled lawyer. You have nothing in common with them," Tyler replied.

Kelsey giggled. "If you think the people of Port Townsend are sweet and friendly, you haven't met Roxy," she commented. She took another *karaage*, and Tyler took a second plate of *karaage* from the conveyor belt.

"There. That one's for you," he said.

"Great. Now I have two plates," Kelsey said. The server arrived with two glasses of water, which she set in front of them.

"Thanks," Tyler said, picking his up and drinking it as the server walked off. "Do I get to keep this?" he asked, tipping the glass of water at Kelsey.

"Until I get thirsty," Kelsey replied. "The chicken's a little salty, so you might want to drink quick."

Tyler took a large drink of the water, and set the half-empty glass in front of himself. He looked back at the conveyor belt and removed a plate of sashimi. He picked up a piece with his chopsticks and instead of eating it, offered it to Kelsey. She ate it off his chopsticks.

"Salmon," she said, once she finished chewing it. "Delicious."

"Don't say I never gave you anything," Tyler commented.

"You could give me a billion dollars," Kelsey teased.

"It would be wasted on you. What would you even do with it? At least Ryan would squander it on interesting things," Tyler said.

"It's wasted on you too," Kelsey commented. "What do you buy except books and chocolate?"

"Good point," Tyler said, eating a piece of the salmon.

"What are you going to do with two billion dollars?" Kelsey asked him, eating another piece of the chicken.

Tyler shook his head. "Leave it to my kids, I guess," he said, shrugging. "Or give it to charity."

"The irony," Kelsey said, since Lisa Olsen had originally planned to give Tyler's money to charity in the first place.

"Tell me about it."

"You could be like Bob."

"Get married a dozen times?" Tyler quipped.

"No, buy a plane."

"A plane doesn't cost a billion dollars." Tyler said.

"How much is one?" Kelsey asked. The fried chicken was really delicious.

"Bob's? Maybe twenty-five million?" Tyler said.

"That won't make a dent," Kelsey mused.

"Nope," Tyler said.

Kelsey took a plate of California rolls off the conveyor belt.

"I guess you can afford this then," she said, winking at him and eating a roll.

"I think so," Tyler said, taking a California roll off her plate and eating it.

"I think you can afford to get your own plate," Kelsey said in mock outrage.

"But yours is right here," Tyler said charmingly.

"You're going to be like that, I see," Kelsey said.

"Like what?" Tyler asked, taking another California roll.

"If you don't stop, I'm going to sue you," Kelsey threatened.

"For what?"

"Theft," Kelsey said.

"It's mine. I can't steal it. I think you should have been listening more carefully when we discussed community property in class," Tyler said. He ate the California roll.

Kelsey giggled.

"You think you're so smart, Tyler Olsen," she said.

"I am. Have you seen my pretty girlfriend?"

"Flatterer."

"Is it working?"

"For what?"

"To stop you from suing me over a plate of California rolls."

"Maybe," Kelsey said. She looked at the conveyor belt. She probably should thank Tyler for eating her food. She was getting to try a lot of new things. She took a plate off the belt.

"Would you like some?" she asked. Tyler shook his head. "What is this?" she asked, taking a closer look at what she had picked.

"Philly roll," Tyler said. Kelsey picked one up with her chopsticks and ate it.

"Not bad," she said.

"I don't think sushi should have cream cheese in it," Tyler commented, looking back at the belt.

"More for me."

"In this case, you're welcome to it," Tyler said. He picked up another plate of avocado rolls. Kelsey finished the Philly rolls, while Tyler finished the plate of avocado rolls. As he was putting his chopsticks to the side of his plate, a chocolate cupcake came into view on the belt. Tyler took it off as it reached him.

"Are you done with sushi already?" Kelsey asked him. She certainly wasn't.

"One should eat dessert first," Tyler said. Kelsey grimaced.

"You're going to eat a cupcake, then go back to sushi?" she asked.

Tyler smiled. "No, I'm saving it for dessert," Tyler said, taking a plate of salmon sushi off of the conveyor belt. "It's the first time I've seen a chocolate cupcake come by us tonight. I thought I'd grab it. Have to strike while the iron is hot. Don't want to miss your chance."

"Then why did it take you over a year to ask me out?" Kelsey asked him.

"Because I knew you loved me," Tyler replied. "I didn't have to ask you out."

Kelsey giggled.

"I believe I used the word arrogant tonight, but I'm not sure it's strong enough," she commented.

"You're my girlfriend now, aren't you? I asked you at the perfect time," Tyler said. Kelsey leaned over and kissed his cheek.

"You keep believing that," she said.

"Fine, when should I ask you to marry me?" Tyler asked, picking up the salmon sushi, and looking at her.

"Are you kidding me?" Kelsey asked him.

"No. You'll turn me down if I ask too early, but I certainly don't want to wait until it's too late," Tyler replied. He ate the salmon.

"It's too early to be thinking of marriage," Kelsey said.

"Ryan doesn't think so," Tyler replied.

"Ryan doesn't have any sense," Kelsey said. She took a piece of salmon and ate it.

Tyler laughed. "That may be true, but on the other hand, Ryan's happy."

"Ignorance is bliss," Kelsey said.

"So what does that make intelligence? Misery?" Tyler asked her. "Anyway, stop changing the subject."

"What subject?" Kelsey asked innocently.

"The subject of our impending marriage," Tyler said.

"You're crazy, you know that?" Kelsey said.

"I can't make you happy. I leave you alone, you're upset because I won't ask you on a date. I date you, you're upset because I want to marry you. I can't win," Tyler said.

"It's too early, I said," Kelsey said.

"I suppose you did," Tyler said, removing a second chocolate cupcake from the conveyor belt and placing it in front of Kelsey.

"Thanks," she said. She removed a plate of tuna sushi from the conveyor belt and ate one.

"Are you really dreading working for Tactec that much?" she asked him.

"What do you mean?"

"That you have to distract yourself by thinking about getting married."

Tyler shook his head.

"Not getting married," he said, correcting her. "Getting married to you."

"Fine. You aren't allowed to ask me while we're in school," Kelsey said, picking up a piece of sushi with her chopsticks. "If we're still together after that, the ball's in your court, and you can ask me whenever you want to." She ate the sushi.

"'If we're still together,'" Tyler repeated.

"You might meet someone else," Kelsey said.

"I won't," Tyler replied. "I was lucky to find you."

"You didn't find me. I sat next to you," Kelsey retorted.

"Same difference," Tyler replied. He picked up a piece of her tuna sushi and ate it.

"Now can we stop talking about getting married?"

"For now," Tyler replied. He placed the chopsticks on an empty plate. "I'm done, except for the cupcake. How about you?"

Kelsey picked up the cupcake and placed it in front of Tyler. She was full.

"Have a cupcake, Tyler."

"That's not what I want," Tyler said. Kelsey looked at the smile on his face.

"But that's what you get," Kelsey said. Then she took a bite of the cupcake.

Tyler surveyed her with his eyes. Kelsey felt herself blushing.

"First you steal my heart. Now you steal my cupcake," he said, kissing her.

"Community property," Kelsey replied, taking another bite.

As they left their apartment building on Monday, Kelsey was surprised to see two people standing outside. As soon as they saw Tyler, they called to him.

"Mr. Olsen!"

Kelsey hesitated, but Tyler stepped boldly forward. Kelsey glanced at the writing pad in one of their hands. They were reporters.

"The *Wall Street Journal* is reporting that your mother had dinner with Richard Kinnon last week," one of them said to Tyler.

"I have no idea who my mother is having dinner with. But I know who I'm having lunch with," Tyler said.

"Do you have any comment?" the other reporter asked.

"None," Tyler said, walking past them. He and Kelsey were quiet until they walked onto campus.

"What was that?" Tyler asked thoughtfully.

"Your mom having dinner with Kinnon?" Kelsey asked.

Tyler shook his head. "I knew about that. I mean how did they know where I live? I need to talk to Jeffrey," Tyler pulled out his phone and sent a message. He received one almost instantly.

"He's coming to campus. Sorry," Tyler said.

"It's okay. I like Jeffrey."

"I like Jeffrey too, but I'm supposed to be having lunch with you."

"You still are," Kelsey replied.

She and Tyler got lunch, and sat at a table overlooking the lake and began to eat. Much sooner than she expected, Jeffrey arrived. To her surprise, Jeffrey was wearing casual clothes. She had never seen him in anything but a suit.

"Is it his day off?" she asked.

"Jeffrey doesn't have days off," Tyler replied. Jeffrey sat down at the table.

"Well?" Tyler said. Jeffrey looked unhappy.

"Tactec security is looking into it."

"I don't want to be ambushed while I'm heading for class," Tyler commented.

"I know," Jeffrey replied.

"We'll need a different place next year," Tyler said. "Maybe a house?"

Jeffrey nodded.

"Couldn't it have been coincidence?" Kelsey asked.

"Only the landlord and Tactec know we're in that building, unless someone's been following me or Ryan, which I think is unlikely," Tyler replied.

"A student could have told them," Jeffrey commented.

"It's possible," Tyler said.

"I'll take care of it," Jeffrey said, rising.

"Thank you," Tyler replied.

"Do you need anything?"

"No, thank you," Tyler smiled. "Is Ryan's apartment ready for the summer?"

"Almost," Jeffrey said, glancing at Kelsey.

"Ready?" Kelsey asked.

"We had to make a few adjustments for Miss Hunter," Tyler commented.

"Jess?" Kelsey asked.

"Locks."

"Oh," Kelsey giggled. Jessica wanted to be able to lock her bedroom door, to discourage late night visits from Ryan.

"It will be ready on time," Jeffrey said. "I'll get back to you about what security finds out. Did you want to visit the house before I rent it for next year?" Jeffrey asked. Tyler shook his head.

"You know what we want. Five bedrooms."

"At least," Jeffrey said. "I'll be in touch. Good day, Kelsey," he said, and he left them.

On Tuesday, Kelsey ate lunch by herself in the dining hall. Ryan had taken Jessica out to lunch, she suspected that Zach was still asleep since he didn't have class until one, and of course, Tyler was working on Law Review. She hadn't seen him since lunch yesterday, when he had been fuming because of the reporters who had interrupted his day.

As she flipped through the day's headlines, one caught her eye, and she pulled up the article:

After the breakup that rocked Seattle, signs of a reconciliation

Seattle-

Less than three weeks after tech giant Tactec settled their overbilling lawsuit against the remains of what had been Seattle's third-largest law firm, Kinnon Martins, two allies turned enemies sat down to break bread together.

At the chic Bellevue eatery, The Forge, Tactec CEO Lisa Olsen was spotted having dinner with Richard Kinnon, the former managing partner of Kinnon Martins on Sunday night.

Ms. Olsen, dressed in a black wrap dress and Mr. Kinnon, who was dressed casually, spent two hours sharing plates of hors d'oeuvres and laughing with each other.

The carefree dinner was a sharp contrast from the past year, where Tactec accused Kinnon Martins of overbilling for work, Kinnon Martins collapsed — putting hundreds of lawyers out of work — and Ms. Olsen sued the Kinnon family personally for defamation. In fact, Mr. and Mrs. Kinnon filed for bankruptcy during the proceedings.

However, all of that seemed to be far behind them as Ms. Olsen and Mr. Kinnon enjoyed a plate of the Forge's signature bacon-wrapped olives.

Surprised onlookers, many of whom have followed the lawsuit closely over the past year, snapped photos, posted on social media and speculated on why Ms. Olsen and Mr. Kinnon selected such a public place for their meeting.

"They both live in Medina and probably Mr. Kinnon could walk to Ms. Olsen's home," said stockbroker Dave Nelson. "Clearly Ms. Olsen wanted to make a statement."

Samantha Turner, a Bellevue secretary, wrote on her Facebook account, "It's been an hour and a half, and they're still acting like best friends. What happened? Was the lawsuit some kind of joke?"

Ms. Turner also posted a photo of Ms. Olsen smiling with the caption, 'WTF? Lisa Olsen and Richard Kinnon aren't at each other's throats?'"

Although the final settlement between Tactec and Kinnon Martins is not public, Tactec commentators theorize that Mr. Kinnon was absolved from responsibility for the overbilling during the suit, and that Ms. Olsen's public meeting was her way of welcoming him back to her good graces.

Since Ms. Olsen has been romantically linked with Seattle attorney Timothy Mayer, and the majority of intellectual property work for Tactec is currently being done his law firm, Taylor, Smart and Mayer, few expect a significant change in the disposition of Tactec's legal work.

However, considering the twenty-year friendship between Ms. Olsen and Mr. Kinnon, which led to the exponential growth of both Tactec and — before its downfall — Kinnon Martins, few are counting Richard Kinnon out of the legal game.

"For two decades, Rich Kinnon was Lisa Olsen's bulldog. They have a lot of history together, live and work in the same town and their sons go to school together. If they can put the past year behind them, they might be a formidable team once again," said Lindi Clark, business reporter for the online Digital Tech Journal.

Neither Ms. Olsen nor Mr. Kinnon were available to comment.

As Kelsey thought about the article, a message came in. It was Alex, messaging her to invite her out to dinner on Thursday night.

Since Law Review didn't close until noon on Friday, Kelsey knew she wouldn't be seeing Tyler for a while. So she decided to accept.

As she replied to Alex, she realized that this was what Tyler had been concerned about when they were in Portland. He was off working, and she was alone, with little to do. And Alex was there.

Although Kelsey knew she was committed to Tyler, and him to her, she could understand how misunderstandings happened.

Misunderstandings like the one that broke up Tyler's family. And, she wondered, perhaps there had been a misunderstanding that had led to the downfall of Richard Kinnon.

"You responded right away," Alex commented as Kelsey put on her seat belt on Thursday. "Broke up with your boyfriend?"

"No, he's busy with Law Review right now."

"Will he be in Seattle this summer?"

"Yes," Kelsey replied.

"Did you tell him that you won't be seeing him because I'm going to make you stay in the office sixteen hours a day?" Alex asked as he started up the car.

"No. I'm confident he'll be working harder than I will. He's working at Simon and Associates."

"Another one from Simon and Associates?" Alex asked.

"I'm going out with Tyler Olsen, Alex," Kelsey replied.

Alex turned his head and looked at Kelsey for what felt to her like a full minute. "Are you kidding me?" he finally said.

"What?"

"Aren't you bored to death?" Alex asked, finally driving off.

Kelsey giggled. "No."

"Right. I think all that money is turning your head," Alex commented.

"Why does everyone assume Tyler's boring?" Kelsey said. "Tyler is a sweetheart."

"I'm sure. I'm surprised he managed to get up the nerve to ask you out. You're so feisty."

"It did take him a while," Kelsey admitted.

"How long have you been dating?"

"Since December," Kelsey replied.

"Interesting. And what does Queen Lisa think of the relationship?"

Kelsey shrugged as they drove down Madison. "No idea. I've known Tyler a long time, so she probably doesn't care."

"Oh, I'm sure she does," Alex replied. "But you seem like a nice enough girl."

"I'd like to think so," Kelsey replied. "So where are we going today?"

"Mariners. You like baseball?"

"I do."

"It's the perfect place to discuss business. Lots of downtime. And we have a lot to discuss."

"Do we?" Kelsey asked.

"Now that I know that you won't see your boyfriend all summer since he'll be trapped in Bill Simon's office, I'll find even more for you to do," Alex said, smiling at her.

As they sat in their seats, Kelsey was wearing a brand new pink Mariners hat she had just bought on the walk to the seats. While they were eating chili fries, Alex explained what he had planned for her for the summer. With one eye on the game, Alex spoke.

"So we're getting another bite at the apple. Rumor has it that Lewis and Lindsay is at maximum capacity doing the Tactec patent work, so Tactec will be inviting a select group of firms in town to make a proposal to do a bunch of additional licensing work from Chen Industries."

"Really?" Kelsey said. "And Collins Nicol is one of them?" she asked.

"It looks like it. We'll get final word in June, and start getting the proposal together in July. Lisa Olsen herself is expected to sit in on the presentations in August. "

"No way."

"It's a lot of billables for whoever wins it," Alex said. "I guess she doesn't trust anyone else to make the decision for her."

"That's exciting," Kelsey said.

"Nerve-wracking. Mary says if we get selected, she wants me to do our presentation."

"Wow."

"Which of course means, you'll be helping me gather everything. So don't expect to have a lot of time off in July."

Kelsey bit her lip. Jasmine's wedding and the Tactec event were both in July.

"Will I have weekends off?" she asked.

"Of course, I'm not a slave driver," Alex said dismissively. He ate a chili fry. "So in addition to the Tactec presentation, I'm going to have you do first drafts of all of the licensing contracts that come in during the summer."

"Seriously?" Kelsey said in surprise. That was a lot of responsibility.

"Sure. I want to enjoy my summer. Maybe I'll find a girlfriend," Alex replied with a grin. "It won't be too bad for you. I have a lot of licensing contracts that you can use as a starting point."

Kelsey nodded.

"And of course, David wants you back. He's got some particularly bad cases he plans on foisting onto your desk."

Kelsey sighed. David Lim did have a lot of complex, annoying cases that were also usually obvious losers for the client. At least he was a nice guy.

"You're going to have a great summer," Alex said cheerfully.

"Done," Tyler said happily, sitting at the lunch table on Friday afternoon. Brandon sat next to him and put his head down on the table. The last issue of Law Review had been sent to the printer, and Tyler and Brandon were free again.

"If you do this to me next year, I'm going to kill you," Brandon said to Tyler.

"I'll prepare to die then," Tyler replied.

"You're going to be worse than Sophia and Christian put together," Brandon said.

"Probably," Tyler replied. "I'll buy your lunch. What do you want?"

"Prime rib," Brandon said. Tyler looked across the table at Kelsey, who smiled at him.

"I think there's tuna casserole," she said to Brandon.

"Fine. Whatever. Just wake me up when you're back."

Kelsey stood. "I'll help you carry," she said to Tyler. She walked over to him. Tyler put his arm around her waist, and they walked to the cafeteria.

"How was it?" she asked.

"It's over. That's all that matters," Tyler replied. "We're having a party next week. Want to go?"

"Sure," Kelsey said. Tyler leaned over and kissed her on the lips.

"I missed you," he said.

"I missed you too," Kelsey replied.

Tyler released her waist, and they began walking through the line. Kelsey selected lasagna for Brandon, and Tyler got the same for himself. As they waited to pay, Tyler asked her, "So what did you do while I was trapped?"

"Studied. Hung out with Jess and Ryan. Got my summer marching orders from Alex."

Tyler looked at her as they moved up in line. "Alex."

"I knew you'd fixate on that one," Kelsey replied.

"Where did he take you?"

"Mariners," she replied.

"I'm not going to be happy this summer, am I?" Tyler said. "You working late nights with Alex Carsten."

"Like it matters. You'll be working too."

"You know what I mean, Miss North," Tyler said, pulling out his wallet and paying for lunch.

Kelsey picked up the tray and she and Tyler began heading back to the table.

"Alex is my boss and that's all," she replied.

"I still intend to be irrationally jealous," Tyler said.

Kelsey giggled. "If you want to, that's fine," she replied.

"I'm glad you agree," Tyler said, stifling a yawn as they reached the table. Kelsey placed Brandon's tray in front of him. He was fast asleep.

"Wake up," Tyler said, putting his on tray down and giving Brandon a shove.

"What? Oh, thanks," Brandon said, seeing the food.

"So what will you be doing with Mr. Carsten?" Tyler asked her, sitting down and picking up his fork. "Wait, I didn't like the sound of that. What will Alex have you working on?" Tyler rephrased. He winked at her.

Kelsey frowned. "Alex will have me do first drafts of the licensing agreements that come in this summer. Plus if Collins Nicol is invited, I'll help Alex with the Tactec presentation."

"Tactec presentation?" Tyler asked. "What Tactec presentation?"

Kelsey looked at him in surprise. She knew something about Tactec that Tyler didn't? That was a first.

"Tactec is going to invite a bunch of law firms to make proposals for the licensing work that Lewis and Lindsay can't handle. Alex will do the Collins Nicol presentation," Kelsey explained.

"Is Lewis and Lindsay turning down work?" Tyler asked Brandon.

"I heard they don't want to hire anyone else right now. Lisa is too capricious. The partners are afraid they'll get a bunch of new staff, and Lisa will pull the work from us," Brandon said sleepily, cutting into his lasagna with his fork.

"She won't, but okay," Tyler said, taking a bite of his own food. "I'll have to ask Ryan who's going to select the winning proposal."

"Alex said that Lisa will be at the presentations."

Tyler shook his head. "That's too low-level for her. Maybe she'll see the last couple, but someone else has got to make the first cut. How many law firms are being invited to make proposals?"

"Alex didn't know, but he thought about ten," Kelsey replied.

"Lisa's not going to sit through ten presentations," Tyler said confidently.

"Do you think she'll send Ryan?" Kelsey asked.

"No," Tyler said. "Ryan might fall asleep. Maybe it will be Tactec's senior counsel," he mused.

"That makes sense," Kelsey replied.

"So he's planning on keeping you busy?" Tyler asked.

"Alex? He said he was."

"I bet," Tyler said.

"Tyler," Kelsey scolded.

"I told you. Irrationally jealous," Tyler replied, biting into his breadstick.

"Kelsey, how do you get a passport? Didn't you just get one?" Morgan asked. She had called Kelsey out of the blue on Friday afternoon. Tyler had left lunch and gone to his apartment to sleep.

"I ordered it, and I'll get it in a few weeks. It isn't hard. The information's online. I can help you," Kelsey replied.

"Thanks."

"Are you going somewhere?" Kelsey asked Morgan.

"It was suggested to me that if I had a passport, I might," Morgan replied mysteriously.

"I see," Kelsey said. She paused. "Should I guess who made the suggestion?"

"I'm guessing you know."

"I'm guessing I do," Kelsey said.

On Saturday, as Kelsey and Jess were sitting in the living room studying, Jessica's phone rang. She glanced at it, answered it and put it on speaker.

"Hi, Andrea," she said.

"Hi, Jessie," Andrea said softly. "Joey's home, but I needed to pass on a message from you from your mother. You know she can't call you."

"I know."

Andrea sighed. "I know that Joey knows I'm in touch with you, but he's not going to say anything to me."

"What's the message?" Jessica asked.

"She told me to tell you that your father expects a phone call from you. This week. Telling him that you're sorry and that you'll be back in New York after your final exam."

"Not going to happen," Jessica said.

"Jessie. Your father said that if you don't call him by the end of this week, he's going to wash his hands of you. I told you. He's got the support of your uncles as well."

"Fine, he can do what he likes," Jessica said bravely. But Kelsey could hear the fear underneath her words.

"Jessie...." Andrea began, but Jessica cut her off.

"Is he coming out here?" Jessica asked.

"No, I don't think so. Your mother said he's got patients booked through July."

"Then I don't see the problem."

"Jess, your mother doesn't know what he's planning to do. He won't tell her. He said that he's ending this one way or another. Either you come back now, or you never come back."

Kelsey felt her heart stop. But Jessica simply twirled a curly strand of hair on her finger.

"Jessica, I will always be your sister-in-law. No, your sister. And your friend. No matter what. But you need to understand what's going on here. Nana believes that your father isn't kidding around."

"My father doesn't know how to kid around," Jessica commented.

"Are you really willing to do this? Leave your family behind?" Andrea said.

"I'm not leaving them behind, I'm moving forward. On my own terms, not Daddy's," Jessica said. "Andrea, I don't want to leave Darrow just because he says so. It's the stepping stone to my future. To fulfilling my dreams. He doesn't understand that because he's too busy trying to hold me under his thumb."

"Are you going to be okay without them? Without us?" Andrea asked.

"If I have to," Jessica replied, biting her lip. "I don't want to leave, but I can't stay like this. Trapped like a prisoner. I've done everything he's wanted me to do until now. But I can't live my life like this. I just can't."

"I know," Andrea sighed. "I am so sorry this is happening to you, Jessica."

There was silence for a moment, then Jessica asked, "Andrea?"

"Yes?"

"Am I right?" Jessica asked her.

There was a long moment of silence, then finally Andrea spoke.

"Yes," she said. "Yes, you are."

"Oh, you look so cute!" Jessica said to Tyler when the boys picked them up on Tuesday.

"You're supposed to say that to me," Ryan pouted.

"You aren't wearing the gorgeous Norwegian flag scarf," Jessica pointed out.

"Celebrating my heritage," Tyler said. Kelsey touched the red, white and blue scarf. It was very soft wool.

"Now I want one," Ryan said.

"You aren't Norwegian," Jessica pointed out.

"I'm an honorary Norwegian. Margaret said so," Ryan said.

"We'll get you a flag. Come on," Tyler said.

"Security is going crazy today," Tyler commented as they walked toward Market Street an hour later. "They really can't protect her well in this crowd."

"Protect her from what?" Kelsey asked.

"There have still been quite a few protests at her speeches because of the trusts," Tyler said as they turned onto Market.

"Is she worried?" Kelsey asked.

"Lisa's like you. Fearless," Tyler replied.

"Where's my flag?" Ryan asked Tyler.

"Look around. We're going to look for food," Tyler replied. He took Kelsey's hand and they began walking through the crowd that lined both sides of the street. Kelsey was fascinated as they walked down the sidewalk. She had no idea that the parade was so popular. There were people as far as she could see.

"What kind of food are we looking for?" Kelsey asked Tyler. "Lutefisk?"

"Absolutely not. Hot dogs," he replied.

"Hot dogs?"

"Norwegian hot dogs," Tyler clarified.

"Okay," Kelsey said doubtfully. They walked several more paces, then Tyler stopped. He had found the hot dog stand. They got in line.

"What's on top?" she asked.

"Fried onions," Tyler replied. "You want to try one, right?"

"Of course," Kelsey replied.

Once they reached the beginning of the line, Tyler got two hot dogs. He picked up two napkins, and handed one to Kelsey, along with her hot dog, which was smothered in crispy brown onion bits.

"Håper at det smaker." Tyler said.

Kelsey looked at him.

"It means *bon appetit*. Wait, that's French," Tyler laughed.

"It's okay. I can translate that," Kelsey said. She took a bite of the hot dog, which was delicious.

"Do you like it?" Tyler asked expectantly.

"It's excellent," Kelsey replied. She and Tyler, along with many other people, stood on the sidewalk, eating their hot dogs and waiting for the parade to start.

Kelsey finished her hot dog, a few seconds after Tyler. He leaned over and kissed her.

"*Jeg elsker deg,*" he said. "I love you."

Ryan and Jessica walked up to them much later. The parade had begun. Ryan waved a red, white and blue Norwegian flag at them.

"Found it!" he said happily.

"This is so fun," Jessica said. She had tied a red, white and blue ribbon around her ponytail.

"What did you eat?" Ryan asked Tyler, over the sound of a high school marching band passing in front of them.

"Hot dogs, of course," Tyler replied.

"Of course," Ryan said.

"Have you had them?" Kelsey asked.

"Margaret made me try it once," Ryan replied.

"It's cultural," Tyler said to him.

"So's lutefisk, but I don't see you eating it," Ryan replied.

"You have a point."

"What is lutefisk, and why are you so against it?" Jessica asked.

"Cod soaked in lye," Tyler said. "I'm sorry for being a bad Norwegian, but I just don't like it that much."

"I'm telling Margaret," Ryan teased.

"She already knows," Tyler replied.

"Have you seen her?" Jessica asked.

"In this crowd. No way," Tyler replied.

"She's probably at the Lodge anyway," Ryan commented.

"Where?" Kelsey asked.

"The Leif Erikson Lodge. It's a couple of streets away. It's like a Norwegian cultural center," Tyler explained.

"There's a lot of Norwegians here in Seattle," Jessica commented.

"We're in Ballard. It's the center of Scandinavian culture in Seattle," Tyler replied. "I think we're getting near the end of the parade," he commented.

Kelsey turned her eyes back to the parade. She had been surprised by the number of bands and groups that had been in the parade. It was certainly a popular event.

Tyler was correct about the parade ending. Kelsey spotted the Grand Marshal's car, with Lisa Olsen sitting in the back of a convertible, perched on the edge between the trunk of the car, and the top of the back seats, so she was very clearly visible.

Lisa Olsen wore a beautiful traditional Norwegian *bunad,* her signature red on top and a bright blue skirt below. The outfit was punctuated with silver jewelry. Her dark hair was flowing over her shoulders and she was smiling.

"Look at her beautiful costume," Kelsey said to Jessica.

"Wow," Jessica commented. "She looks amazing."

Ryan took a photo as the car slowly passed by them. Kelsey spotted a lot of very nervous looking men walking next to the car, and looking into the crowd. Tactec security, she imagined. The car headed down Market Street and turned onto 24th, heading toward the end.

"That's it," Tyler said, as the crowds slowly began to disburse.

"That was amazing," Jessica said. "Thank you for bringing us."

"Yeah, that was great. Thanks," Kelsey said.

"I'm glad you enjoyed it," Tyler said. "Sharing my heritage."

"Better than sharing your lutefisk," Ryan teased.

The boys took the girls to a beautiful Italian restaurant for dinner, a few blocks away, then they drove back home. Ryan and Jessica returned to the apartment building, while Kelsey and Tyler walked over to the park. A few children were playing with their attentive parents keeping an eye on them, and Tyler led Kelsey to a quiet seat away from the playground.

They sat, and Tyler kissed her.

"Jeg…" Kelsey began, but she couldn't remember the words.

"Jeg elsker deg," Tyler coaxed her.

"Jeg els…" Kelsey sighed.

"Jeg elsker deg," Tyler said patiently. Kelsey pouted.

"I love you," she said, kissing him.

"Good enough," Tyler replied, kissing her back.

Now that Law Review was over, Tyler spent several days in Kelsey's apartment trying to catch up. There were moments when Kelsey was wondering exactly he was trying to catch up on, because instead of studying, he seemed to be flirting.

"So are we going for a replay of the last Law Review party?" Tyler teased on Friday night. Kelsey glared at him. They were walking to a small restaurant in Madison Park, where this year's party was being held.

"Absolutely not. I'm not dancing with you," Kelsey replied.

"I was actually thinking about the kiss," Tyler said. Kelsey smiled at him.

"Yeah, the kiss was nice," she admitted.

"I thought about that kiss for weeks," Tyler said.

Kelsey felt her breath quicken. Although she would never admit it to Tyler, so had she.

"Are we really looking for hot pink dresses? This isn't a joke?" Kelsey asked as she, Jasmine, Morgan, and Jessica walked down 4th Avenue late on Saturday morning.

"Not a joke, North," Jasmine said.

Kelsey sighed.

Jasmine and Morgan had arrived in Seattle an hour ago, and they had all driven down for what Kelsey expected would be one of the more unpleasant days of her life.

Morgan glanced at Kelsey. "Give up, Kels. We aren't getting out of this one."

"Have you tried to talk her out of this?" Kelsey demanded.

"Morgan's spent months complaining. I don't care. This is my wedding and you're both wearing pink," Jasmine said.

"I hate you," Kelsey said.

"You do not."

"Okay, I don't. But why, Jazz? What have we done to you?"

"It will be fine. Stop whining," Jasmine said. "We're here," she said brightly. The girls looked up. They had reached the first stop on their whirlwind bridesmaid dress tour. Kelsey sighed again, and Jessica giggled and put her arm around Kelsey's shoulders.

"I'm here for you, Kels," she said.

"If only you could wear the dress for me," Kelsey replied.

Jasmine had helpfully called ahead, so Kelsey and Morgan were able to try on five bright pink dresses in a row.

"It just gets more awful with each one," Morgan said, looking at herself in the mirror.

"Jazz, that color isn't really flattering on either of them," Jessica commented.

"That's the point," Kelsey snapped. Jasmine had a small smile on her lips.

After leaving the bridal salon, the girls headed for a department store with a large array of evening gowns.

"Really? You're going to make us try on more?" Kelsey said.

"I have never known you to complain so much," Jasmine said to her.

"You've never been so mean to me," Kelsey retorted.

"I'm not being mean," Jasmine said. "This is my vision."

"Then get some glasses," Morgan snapped. "We look hideous."

"Maybe a nice red?" Jessica suggested.

"No," Jasmine said firmly.

"Pale pink?" Morgan asked.

Jasmine shook her head.

"Even salmon pink? I'd happily wear salmon pink," Kelsey said.

"Bright pink," Jasmine said.

Kelsey sighed again.

As they entered the department store, Jessica said that she needed to go to the bathroom. While they waited for her, Jasmine leaned against a wall.

"Someone's been to Seattle recently," Jazz commented, looking at Morgan, who grinned.

"Tyler was right. Ryan's house is really, really nice," Morgan said.

Kelsey looked at Morgan. "When were you here?"

"Two weeks ago. Bob flew me over for dinner," Morgan said.

"Really? Are you serious?" Kelsey said. Morgan nodded.

"So how many times have you seen him?" Kelsey asked.

"Three. L.A, Las Vegas, and here in Seattle," Morgan said.

"Once a month," Jazz said.

Morgan shrugged. "He's a busy guy."

"I can't believe you," Jasmine said.

"Don't be a hater, Jazz," Morgan said.

"I'm not. I just, well I don't know."

"Look, we're just having fun. It's not like I'm going to marry him," Morgan said.

"What do you think, Kels?" Jasmine asked.

"I think I don't have an opinion. And you don't need to have one either. It's Morgan's life. Having said that, Bob seems nice enough."

"What does Ryan think about this?" Jasmine asked.

"I don't think Ryan knows a lot about Bob's private life," Kelsey said.

"Wait, he doesn't know?" Jasmine said.

"If he did, I'm not sure he'd care," Kelsey shrugged.

"He wouldn't care that his father was dating someone his age?"

"I'm older than Ryan," Morgan said.

"Barely," Jasmine said.

"Ryan and Bob have dated the same women. Nothing would surprise Ryan," Kelsey said confidently.

The three girls stood quietly until Jessica came out a minute later. "Where next?" she asked.

"To find the perfect dress," Jasmine said brightly. Kelsey and Morgan looked at each other, and frowned.

"So, Jessica, how's Ryan?" Morgan asked as they walked.

"He's fine," Jessica replied.

"He's fine, all right. He's as cute as Tyler," Jasmine said. "When are you going to marry him?"

"After graduation," Jessica said.

Kelsey looked at her with surprise. "You told Ryan two days ago that you weren't marrying him," Kelsey said to her.

"He knows I'm kidding," Jessica replied.

"Why are you waiting?" Jasmine asked. "If you know you want to marry him, why not get married now?"

"In school?" Jessica asked.

"Why not?" Jasmine said. "It only takes an afternoon to get married."

"I suppose," Jessica said. "We can wait."

"I'm not sure Tyler can," Morgan commented. Jasmine and Jessica giggled.

"What do you mean?" Kelsey asked her.

"Tyler's obsessed with you," Jessica commented.

"He is not," Kelsey said dismissively.

"Kelsey's like a tiny bunny rabbit in a field, eating a blade of grass, who doesn't notice the giant wolf slowly circling her, waiting for his chance," Morgan giggled.

"The way Tyler looks at you with those chocolate brown eyes. I thought he was going to start a forest fire when we were camping," Jasmine said.

"Don't be ridiculous," Kelsey said.

"Kelsey's oblivious," Morgan said, shaking her head.

"You just don't notice, Kels," Jessica added. "Tyler looks at Kelsey, bites his lip, sighs, looks away, then his eyes slowly move right back to her again. If it was anyone but Tyler, I'd say you better get a double lock on your bedroom door this summer."

"You three are crazy," Kelsey said.

"Not as crazy as Tyler is about you," Jasmine said.

"It doesn't matter. I'm certainly not getting married any time soon," Kelsey said.

"Yeah, Tyler's too busy to ask you," Jessica agreed. "I will never understand the two of you."

"We have things to do," Kelsey said.

"You could add getting married to that list," Jasmine pointed out.

"Tyler has to ask me first," Kelsey said.

"You know he wants to," Jessica said.

Kelsey sighed. "It's like us going out on a date. I'm not going to push him," she said to Jessica.

"Has he told you he wants to get married?" Jasmine asked.

"Perhaps," Kelsey said.

"Has he asked you?" Morgan asked.

"No," Kelsey laughed.

"Don't say no if he does, North," Jasmine warned.

"He's not going to ask me. Not for a long time," Particularly since she had told him not to, she thought.

"Tyler thinks you're going to wait around forever," Jessica said, shaking her head.

"Tyler knows I love him," Kelsey said. The other three looked at her in surprise.

"What did you just say?" Jasmine said.

"OMG," Jessica said.

"Kelsey admitted that she loves Tyler?" Morgan said.

"So?" Kelsey shrugged, but she could feel herself blushing. Her admission had just slipped out of her mouth, and there was no getting out of it now.

"No wonder Tyler waited so long. He knows he's got your heart locked up," Jessica said happily.

"Forget what I said," Kelsey grinned.

"No, no way. We're holding you to that," Jasmine said.

"At Thanksgiving, you would barely say that you liked him," Morgan pointed out.

"It's been six months," Kelsey said. "Tyler's special to me. But it doesn't matter. He's not going to ask me any time soon. Anyway, whoever marries Tyler is going to have a lot of responsibilities just being his wife. He's probably going to be CEO of Tactec in the next five to ten years.

"I came to Darrow to have a career of my own, and I'm not planning on giving that up, no matter how much I love him. So if he does ask me, I've got a lot to consider."

"What about you, Jess? Is that a problem for you?" Jasmine asked.

Jessica shook her head. "I want a career, but I'm not as driven as Kels. Anyway, Ryan's not going to be CEO. Whatever he does at Tactec, he'll have plenty of time for me. Tyler barely has time for Kelsey now."

"Exactly," Kelsey said.

Jasmine pouted. "I just want to see you happy."

"I am happy," Kelsey said.

"Happily married," Jasmine clarified.

"One day, Jazz," Kelsey said.

"You promise? I don't want to find out you turned down a proposal," Jasmine commented.

Kelsey giggled. "I won't tell you," she said.

"You will too," Jasmine pouted as they entered the dress department.

"Not if you put me in a bright pink dress. Because then our friendship will be over," Kelsey said, as Morgan began looking through the racks.

"I don't know why you're over there looking at black and navy dresses, Morgan Hill," Jasmine said to her. "The bright colors are over here."

Morgan frowned and joined the others. Jasmine pulled a bright pink monstrosity off the display.

"I think you're joking with them," Jessica said, looking at the dress in Jasmine's hand.

"Unfortunately, you haven't known Jasmine as long as we have," Kelsey commented.

"She's serious," Morgan agreed.

Jasmine looked through the dresses, a determined look on her face. Kelsey and Morgan hung back, waiting to be told what to try on next.

"This one," Jasmine said in triumph, pulling a sleek fuchsia sheath dress off the rack. It had a thin belt with a rhinestone buckle. "Try this one," she said, handing one dress to Morgan, and the other to Kelsey. Both girls sighed, but they took the dresses and trudged to the fitting room.

"Why, Kels?" Morgan called over the dressing room wall.

"I have no idea," Kelsey said, looking at her reflection in the mirror. Although the dress style was beautiful, the color was completely wrong for her skin tone. She looked pale and horrible. She stepped out of the dressing room. Morgan stood there, frowning at her own reflection.

"Let's show her," Kelsey said in defeat. She and Morgan returned to Jessica and Jasmine.

"That's it!" Jasmine said happily. She snapped a photo of the two of them with her phone. She walked around them, looking carefully at the dresses.

"Jazz, the color makes them look like they haven't seen the sun in months. Or years," Jessica said. "Although the style is beautiful on both of you."

The saleswoman walked over. She lifted her eyebrows when she saw Kelsey and Morgan, but said nothing.

"Can I help you?" she asked.

"Do these come in a different color?" Morgan asked hopefully. Jasmine glared at her.

"It comes in navy, black, and also a bright green." the saleswoman replied. "With your coloring, the navy would be quite flattering." Kelsey and Morgan looked at Jasmine.

"We'll take the pink," Jasmine interjected. "Get changed."

Morgan, Jessica, and Kelsey watched helplessly as Jasmine walked over to the counter to pay for the dresses. Morgan sighed, and she and Kelsey returned to the dressing room to get changed.

When they returned, they expected Jasmine to take the dresses they were holding, but instead she was holding a receipt.

"They will send new ones to me. I don't want to buy the ones off the rack. They might have gotten damaged."

Morgan and Kelsey handed the pink dresses to the smiling salesclerk as Jasmine securely placed the receipt into her purse.

"They fit perfectly, so make sure you don't gain weight," Jasmine warned as they walked out of the department.

"That's a great idea," Kelsey said to Morgan.

"I was hoping that they'd get lost in the mail," Morgan said. "Maybe I can wait outside the house and tackle the postman."

"So how much do we owe you to look miserable?" Kelsey said.

"You mean to look beautiful. One hundred and forty five dollars with tax," Jasmine said brightly.

"At least you don't have to have them altered," Jessica said.

"Yeah, that's fabulous," Morgan said without enthusiasm.

"I'm buying your shoes for you," Jasmine said.

"Thank you," Kelsey said.

"Thanks, Jazz," Morgan said glumly.

"It's my pleasure," Jasmine smiled.

As they headed into the last weeks of school, Kelsey spent a lot of time studying licensing with Tyler. As Lisa Olsen's son, Tyler was quite confident around any and all contracts that took technology from one company, and allowed a second company to use it.

"Why do so many of our examples use King County as the venue for lawsuits?" Kelsey asked.

"Because a lot of tech companies are in Seattle," Tyler said.

"A lot are in California too," Kelsey said.

"Yes, but California law has a reputation for being more consumer-friendly than pretty much every other state in the nation. Also, since so many of the big companies are here, they insist on litigating locally. All Tactec contracts require lawsuits to be brought in King County."

"Even if the other company is overseas?"

"Especially then. No one wants to hire counsel in Amsterdam, or Romania, or wherever a tiny software company is located."

"Like Taipei," Kelsey said, referencing Chen Industries.

"Exactly. Taiwanese law, and everything's in Chinese? My mother would fire any lawyer who agreed to that. Just to file the lawsuit is going to cost you thousands of extra dollars."

"No wonder there's so much IP work in Seattle," Kelsey said thoughtfully.

"Perfect for you," Tyler said.

"I guess," Kelsey said.

"And me," Tyler replied.

"Why?"

"If you stay in IP, you'll stay in Seattle."

"I could move to California."

"No one wants to move to California," Tyler said.

Kelsey giggled. "Ryan does."

"Only because it's hot. Ryan's not moving anywhere. He's going to be right here, stuck with me."

"Lucky him," Kelsey said.

Tyler glanced at her. "Are you suggesting that you would like to be here, stuck with me too?"

"I didn't say that," Kelsey teased.

"You think you're being coy, but I know you like me," Tyler said.

"I don't know why you'd think that," Kelsey said haughtily.

"No?" Tyler said, moving closer to her.

"No."

"Here's why," Tyler said, leaning over and kissing her deeply.

Kelsey took a breath when Tyler finally broke away.

"Just because you're a good kisser doesn't mean I like you," she said.

"I'm not just a good kisser, Kelsey," Tyler said. He allowed the comment to hang in the air for a moment. "I'm also an excellent law student. So we need to get back to work." he continued.

"Or?" Kelsey asked.

"Don't tease me, Miss North," Tyler warned.

"You tease me all of the time," Kelsey said. "You're a big flirt."

"Am I?" Tyler asked in amusement.

"Yes. So I can flirt with you too," Kelsey replied.

"No, you can't," Tyler said seriously. "I don't have your self-control."

"Of course you do."

"Kelsey, how many times have we had to leave an apartment because you were flirting with me?"

Kelsey thought about the question.

"It's been a couple of times at least," she admitted.

"So no flirting," Tyler said.

Kelsey pouted.

Tyler looked away from her. "Stop it," he said.

Kelsey put her iPad on the table and moved so she was directly in his line of vision.

"Am I distracting you, Mr. Olsen?" she asked saucily.

"I've warned you," Tyler said to her.

"Right," Kelsey said scornfully. She reached for her iPad, but without warning, Tyler grabbed her around her waist and pulled her toward himself. He kissed her passionately, and Kelsey felt herself get hot. His lips lingered on hers.

Tyler broke away after a long moment, and looked into her eyes. Kelsey looked back. She had seen this fire in Tyler's eyes several times, and it was back.

"Don't tease me, Kelsey," he whispered. It sounded like a plea.

"I won't," Kelsey replied seriously. Tyler looked away. "I'm sorry," she added. He nodded.

"You make me crazy," Tyler said softly. He looked at her, and kissed her again.

This time, Kelsey gently pushed him away. He stopped kissing her, but his arm remained around her waist. He ran the fingers of his free hand through her loose hair. Then he released her. He took a deep breath.

"Perhaps," Tyler said thoughtfully, reaching for his own iPad, which was sitting on the coffee table, "Jeffrey needs to put a lock on your door too."

They were about to start their last week of classes for the year, and although there was still plenty of studying to do, both Tyler and Kelsey felt secure enough in their work to go out on a long date on Saturday afternoon.

Tyler had driven them up to Montlake, and they had walked over to the Waterfront Activities Center behind Husky Stadium. Tyler had a surprise for Kelsey.

"I can't believe we're in a canoe," Kelsey said, as they pushed off from shore. Kelsey was really excited. She hadn't been in a canoe in ages.

"It seemed like the kind of thing Miss North would like," Tyler said, from behind her.

"Have you done this before?" she asked him.

"I took sailing lessons, but no," Tyler said.

"You took sailing lessons? You really are a preppy," Kelsey commented.

"I would have rowed crew in college, but they were out on the river at 6 a.m.," Tyler said. "No way was I getting up that early."

"You get up at six now," Kelsey pointed out.

"I get up to see you. If you had been on the crew team, I would have gotten up then too," Tyler replied. Kelsey smiled to herself and paddled gently through the water lilies. It was absolutely beautiful here. The water sparkled in the May sunlight, and although it was still chilly in Seattle, it had warmed up enough that Kelsey felt comfortable in just a long t-shirt. Her fleece was in Tyler's car.

"What were sailing lessons like?"

"Have you ever been dumped into the frigid waters of Lake Washington?"

"No."

"It felt like that," Tyler commented. "It was less like sailing and more like trying not to drown."

Kelsey giggled. "Did Ryan go with you?"

"No, Zach. Our mothers thought we'd have fun," Tyler said. "Or they were trying to kill us. I'm not sure which."

Kelsey laughed again, as she felt Tyler steer the boat with his paddle.

"Look, there's a heron. Right side," Kelsey looked up. A giant, stately looking bird stood unmoving on a pylon in the water.

"Beautiful," Kelsey said.

"Yes, you are," Tyler replied. Kelsey was happy her back was to him, because she felt herself blush.

"When will you stop teasing me?" Kelsey asked from the front of the boat.

"Never," Tyler said.

They paddled along the shore, looking at the beautiful plants and the wildlife that flourished by the edge.

"Are you looking forward to living with me again?" Tyler asked.

"Very much," Kelsey said.

"Will you come to Simon's to have dinner with me every night?"

"Most nights," Kelsey said.

"Because some nights Mr. Carsten intends to get in my way," Tyler commented.

"Alex is mentoring me this summer. You should be happy for me. He's a partner now, so it's quite an honor," Kelsey pointed out.

"I suppose," Tyler said doubtfully.

"I came to law school to be a lawyer. I didn't come to Darrow to meet you," Kelsey said.

"You didn't?" Tyler asked in mock surprise. "I came to Darrow to meet you," he teased.

"Well, I am your princess," Kelsey said, as imperiously as possible.

"That you are," Tyler replied. She could hear the smile in his voice.

"I need to start thinking about what I want to do after graduation. We only have a year left," Kelsey said.

"You mean besides marry me?" Tyler said.

"Cut it out, Tyler," Kelsey said.

"I'm just saying, I'm hoping that's part of your plan," Tyler said.

"Like I said, I'm not thinking about marrying you until you ask me."

"After graduation."

"Right."

"With a ring."

"Exactly."

"I thought you weren't like your mother," Tyler said.

"In that respect, I am. The ring proves that you're sincere, and not just kidding around," Kelsey said.

"Is that why Jess wants one? Before she says yes to Ryan?"

"That's why."

"You don't think it's archaic? The man pays for his bride with jewelry?" Tyler asked.

"I think Jess would say that the woman has a lot more to lose, so it's like insurance that the guy is serious."

"Jessica would say that," Tyler admitted. "Does she want to marry Ryan?"

"I think so," Kelsey said. "Does he really want to marry her this year?"

"He says so," Tyler said. "But he doesn't think Jessica will agree."

"She said she wanted to get married after the bar exam," Kelsey said.

"That's what she told Ryan too," Tyler said. "But as we all know, Ryan is impatient."

"Why does he want to get married now?"

"I think he's afraid that Jess will change her mind again. I'm not sure I blame him for worrying. Since they started dating, Jessica's broken up with him once and spent last summer away from him in New York. I think Ryan sees marriage as the only way to keep her with him."

"I guess he has a point," Kelsey agreed. "Does he really want five kids?"

"He does," Tyler said. "At a minimum. Ryan loves kids."

"Do you think he'll stay with Jess?"

"Stay married to her? Of course. Ryan's not Bob," Tyler said. "Ryan wants what he never had, a stable, happy family life. He'll do anything that Jessica wants to make that happen."

"What do you want?" Kelsey asked him.

"Besides you?"

"Yes, besides me."

"I just want to be happy, Kelsey," Tyler said.

After lunch on Wednesday, Tyler and Kelsey walked over to the student mailboxes with Jessica and Ryan. Jessica had got a message telling her that she had received a number of packages and needed to pick them up. Jessica looked in her mailbox and pulled out several paper slips. Each slip represented one package.

"Why do you have so many packages?" Ryan asked Jessica.

"I don't know. I haven't ordered anything. They aren't from you, are they?"

"Nope," Ryan replied.

Jessica handed the slips over to the mail clerk. He glanced at them and proceeded to bring out five large boxes.

"Wow. Are you sure you didn't order anything?" Ryan asked, as he helped Jessica stack the boxes away from the counter.

"No," Jessica said, as Tyler took one of the boxes from her arms. As Ryan took the last one from the mail clerk, Jessica looked at the return.

"They're from home," she said, and she began to open one of the boxes. She pulled off the tape and opened the flaps. Then she gasped and put her hand to her mouth in surprise. Kelsey saw the beginnings of tears as Jessica dashed out of the mailroom.

"Wait. What happened?" Ryan said to Kelsey. Kelsey walked over and looked inside the box. Her shoulders fell as she realized what was inside.

"What's in the box?" Ryan demanded.

"Jessica's things from her room in New York," Kelsey said softly, replacing the flap. "They've thrown her out."

Want my unreleased 5000-word story
Introducing the Billionaire Boys Club
and other free gifts from time to time?

Then join my mailing list at

http://www.caramillerbooks.com/inner-circle/

Subscribe now and read it now!

You can also follow me on Twitter and Facebook

Made in the USA
Middletown, DE
17 October 2023